Bewitched

By

Brenda L. Thomas

Phillywriter LLC

Philadelphia, PA

Bewitched © 2018 by Brenda L. Thomas
Phillywriter, LLC
www.brendalthomas.com
brendalthomas@comcast.net
215-331.4554

First Edition February 2018
ISBN E-book: 978-0-9797622-4-6
ISBN Print: 978-0-9797622-3-9

Manufactured and Printed in the United States of America

Publishers Note:

This novel is a work of fiction. Any references to historical events; to real people, living or dead; or to real locales are intended only to give the fiction a setting in historic reality. Other names, characters, places, and incidents either are the product of the author's imagination or are used fictitiously, and their resemblance, if any, to real-life counterparts is entirely coincidental.

Editor: Lisa C. Miller
Cover Design: Charles A. Preston III | ChaseGFX

Also by Brenda L. Thomas

NOVELS
Woman On Top
Every Woman's Got A Secret

The Velvet Rope
Fourplay, The Dance of Sensuality
Threesome, Where Seduction, Power and Basketball Collide

NON-FICTION
Laying Down My Burdens

SHORT STORIES
Secret Service, An Erotic Short
Every New Year

ANTHOLOGIES
Four Degrees of Heat
Maxed Out

Kiss The Year Goodbye
Every New Year

Bedroom Chronicles
The Experiment

Indulge
The Watcher

Bewitched

Prologue

Dark Shadows

Bryce Goodman

My phone vibrates with a call. I can't answer. I can only stare at the images displayed on the monitor. There's no doubt about what I'm looking at—it's my dick, stuffed in the mouth of my ex-fiancé. Behind her kneels my ex-girlfriend, whose tongue furiously dips in and out the crack of my ex-fiancé's fat ass.

My phone vibrates again.

Confident that whoever is calling is the person responsible for sending the flash drive of the video I'm looking at, I don't answer. Instead, I keep watching. If it were just a sex tape, I wouldn't care. However the footage that follows makes me out to be a sexual predator.

This part of the video shows a man with a predilection for watching women—me—slipping, presumably unnoticed, inside the ladies room of several of Philly's most respected and affluent restaurants. It's never been my desire to approach anyone; in fact it doesn't even get my dick hard. I only wish to observe women at their most vulnerable moments because it provides me with the ability to understand what's really beneath the surface of their public façade. But little did I know someone was watching me.

I uncap a bottle of Macallan M single malt and, foregoing the glass, I turn the bottle up to my lips. As I take a swallow of the warm, smooth liquor, the outside door to my office buzzes.

Tiffany Johnson-Skinner

Did he know I'd come? Maybe that's why his door is unlocked. Now that I'm inside, there's nothing much to see except the basic essentials: a black leather couch, matching recliner and a flat-screen TV mounted on the wall. On the coffee table there are three neatly stacked piles of the *Financial Times*, *The Rake* and *Forbes*. In the kitchen, there are no dirty dishes or signs that he even cooks. I open the refrigerator and see bottles of Poland Spring water and a bag of rotten green apples. His freezer is empty, save for two empty ice trays.

His apartment matches his public persona—nondescript—but I know there's more to Bryce Goodman. Tonight I intend to find out exactly what that is.

With nothing to do but wait, I scramble through my purse for a perfectly rolled Kush. Using his stove to light it, I inhale deeply, filling my lungs and finally my head.

Bryce

Sliding open my bottom desk drawer, I remove my trusted Smith & Wesson pistol and shove it into the waistband of my pants. Standing now, I take another swallow of Macallan then make my way out of my office, through the reception area and to the front door.

I peer over the frosted glass of my storefront window. The black Maybach idling against the curb shines under the streetlight. The driver swings the back door open and a woman dressed in a black pantsuit climbs out, making me realize that a gun isn't what I need.

Raquel Turner-Cosby

Bryce Goodman has never been on my radar and he certainly does not run in my social circle. Clearly, he hides his net worth and a disgusting penchant for voyeurism behind his pristine reputation and no-frills office. That ends tonight.

Swallowing any doubt about confronting him, I step through the doorway of his cramped office. After my eyes adjust to the dark, I maneuver my way around boxes and bins that are haphazardly stacked around the room. Finally, I make out the contour of his body posted against the back counter.

"Did you receive my package?" I ask the shadow lurking in the dark.

I wait for a response. There is none, except him turning a bottle up to his lips. I continue.

"Mr. Goodman, I believe you already know who I am so I will tell you why I'm here. It has come to my attention that my daughter has retained your firm to manage a portion of her investments. I understand that she wants to be independent but I will not allow her, or my wealth, to be mishandled."

Bryce

She is right about one thing—I do know who she is. The woman standing in my office threatening me is Raquel Turner-Cosby who spent four years in federal prison for murdering a man allegedly in self-defense. I also recall meeting with her mixed-race daughter for the first time a few weeks earlier. Apparently the white woman standing before me has a few secrets of her own.

To keep from pulling my gun on her, I turn the bottle up to my lips and take another swallow. She continues to talk but I'm only half listening. Right now Ms. Turner-Cosby is nothing more than a rambling mannequin shrouded in the red light from the glowing Staples sign across the street.

I can't figure out what's more comical, me watching women or this woman hiring someone to watch me watch them. She continues to talk.

Tiffany Johnson-Skinner

Standing in the middle of his neatly organized bedroom, my eyes are drawn to his king-sized bed with its padded gray headboard and nail head trim. I resist the urge to immediately undress and slip between the sheets. Instead, I grab his pillow and breathe in the woody fresh scent of Creed Green Irish Tweed.

Across the room, on his otherwise clean dresser, sits an iPod dock, an envelope stuffed with rolls of 20- and 50-dollar bills wrapped tight in rubber bands and two unique watch boxes. Nestled inside one of them, is an average alligator-strap Rolex etched with his initials. Alongside that lies a not-so-average, blue-faced Piaget. My eyes fixate on a beautiful gold and sapphire-embedded Hublot that looks like it's never even been worn. I turn the key to unlock the box, remove the Hublot and see "10X" etched on the back. I slip it on my wrist. Now I see how he likes to spend his money.

The second box is encased in leather and bares an inscription, "The Good Box." Its contents are more titillating than the watches...a loosely knotted, red silk Hermès men's necktie; I slip that around my neck. Next to it is a packet of Skyn condoms, and Lelo massage candles whose wicks have previously been burned. There's also a fresh tube of L'Occitane almond cream and a velvet sachet that holds a silver pinwheel. All of this affirms my decision to choose Mr. Goodman as the man to handle my finances and hopefully me as well.

Raquel Turner-Cosby

His lack of response is unsettling and so is his constant drinking from that bottle. Maybe I misjudged this man. Is he more of a physical threat then I had assumed? I mean, what person wouldn't be after viewing the images I'd sent him?

"Mr. Goodman, I'm warning you, if you take advantage of my daughter or threaten to expose our personal arrangement in anyway, I will destroy you. I've done it before. And I have no problem accepting the consequences, especially when it comes to my daughter. Are we clear?"

Bryce

Am I drunk, or did this bitch just threaten to kill me? Fuck that.

Reaching behind me, I pull the gun from my waistband then hold it down at my side as I unlatch the safety. When I step back to get my footing, I stumble. Without considering the consequences I say, "Bitch, get the fuck outta my office."

Chapter One

Nightcap

With my head still reeling from what now is a real threat, I stagger up the stairs from my office to my apartment. When I open the door, before I'm able to flip the light switch, a woman's hand covers mine.

"WHO THE FUCK?"

"Welcome home, Bryce. Sorry to startle you."

"Are you crazy? How'd the fuck you get in here?"

"That was the easy part."

Taking the bottle from my hands, she holds it up to my lips and tells me, "You're gonna need to drink all of this."

Even though I can't see her clearly, I know who it is from the scent of her perfume. I swallow too much and it spills out the corners of my mouth. She uses her tongue to lick away the excess.

"Look I can't do....you gotta..."

"There's no such thing as can't, I'm your client."

In the darkened room I can see her in silhouette, sliding her panties down her thighs. She steps out of them and presses her warm body up against me.

I tell myself to focus but my hardened dick confirms I've lost the battle.

"S-h-h-h-h-h," she whispers, then sucks on my middle finger, before pushing it inside her hot pussy that squishes with her juices.

"You don't understand..." I attempt to say but my last few words turn into a mumble when she silences me by swiping that same finger across my top lip, filling my nostrils with the sweet stink of her pussy.

Shit, why had I drunk so much?

Attempting to push her off, I fall backwards, banging my head against the door. She catches me by grabbing my hands, and then she places them on her cotton-soft breasts.

I hear a voice reverberating in my head, "...*take advantage of my daughter... I'll destroy you...*" Would it matter to Ms. Cosby that her daughter is taking advantage of *me* right now?

I feel her unzipping my pants and unfolding my dick from its safe place. My floor creaks when she steps back and drops down to her knees. Her moist lips kiss the head of my dick, licking away the thick cum that has risen to the top and spilled out.

For the last time I ask myself, "What the fuck am I doing? This is the governor's wife, the daughter of the woman who just threatened to blackmail me!" But right now, she's nothing more than a nasty bitch with my dick in her mouth.

Chapter Two

The Hangover

My vibrating phone wakes me from what must be a coma. Straining to squint at the blue screen, I see 37 missed calls, 24 voicemails and 102 text messages.

From a throat filled with what feels like sawdust, I struggle to say, "Bryce...here."

"BOSS, BOSS! WHERE ARE YOU? EVERYBODY'S LOOKING FOR YOU! ARE YOU OKAY? DID YOU LEAVE TOWN? YOU MISSED THREE MEETINGS THIS MORNING."

"Wait, wait... hold on."

I drop the phone and, tripping over the mattress, which has separated from the box spring, I barely make it to the bathroom before vomit spews from my mouth. Overwhelmed by the urge to pee, I grab hold of my limp and incredibly sore dick and release a stream of piss that I've been holding for way too long. Holding onto the wall for support, I make my way back into the bedroom and pick up the phone. That's when I see the lamp on my nightstand is missing its shade and one of the blackout blinds is hanging mangled from the window. The "Good Box" is empty.

"Shanté, stop talking, tell me, what day is it?" I ask, barely able to focus with the bag of bricks banging around in my head.

"Monday, it's Monday afternoon, boss, and we got a ton of work. The phones...."

While Shanté continues to talk, I creep into the living room to find my clothes heaped in a pile at the front door. On top is my gun, the empty bottle of Macallan and a woman's single black stiletto. Who the hell had I been with...Cinderella?

"Shanté, I'm gonna need aspirin and some ice, get me some ice."

Then it all starts to come back to me, at least part of it does. Raquel Turner-Cosby had visited my office... No, the flash drive with that video had arrived first. Had I slept with that woman? No, I was drinking...the daughter, my client; Tiffany Johnson-Skinner had been waiting in my apartment. What had I done to her?

Chapter Three

Risk Management

On my desk Shanté places a large, plastic cup filled with ice, a 32-ounce Pepsi, a 16-ounce Dunkin Donuts coffee and a bottle of Excedrin. I need them all.

Examining me over her glasses, Shanté whispers, "Boss, I gotta admit I ain't never seen you like this. What happened? Did somebody drug you?"

I press the cup of ice against my forehead, swallow four Excedrin and chase them with the Pepsi. This is the second hangover of my life, the last one having been after my high school graduation.

"Tell me what I missed. But Shanté, tell me slowly."

"Okay...so on the concierge side, Mr. Tate wants six orchestra seats for Hamilton; I was able to pull four from last night's auction but I'm not sure I can get the others. I still need six 'cause they wanna sit together but if I get them, I'm sure we can get rid of the four. The Steinways called and they want a four-star package for the British Open. I gave them your price and they said make it happen. Sheem stopped by and left an envelope for you so I put it in the *unlocked safe*,' she says with emphasis, "and he wants 30 VIP tickets with all the trimmings to all the Eagles home and away games, and I also bought up 120 tickets for the Kanye and Jay-Z reunion tour, they just announced it and you know..."

Seeing my distress at her rambling, she stops talking.

"I'm sorry about the safe," I respond, hoping she hasn't seen the flash drive that is still stuck in my computer. "Where's Hampton?" I ask, referring to my business partner and close friend.

"He's at Liberty Place with your mom, they're finishing up. You do remember we're moving, right?"

I nod in agreement.

"Now on the other side of the house..."

"Wait, text Hamp and tell him I said to get the office swept for any type of listening or video recording devices and this place too."

Her raised eyebrows ask why.

"Just do it, Shanté, and also call my housekeeper. I need her to come today. Tell her I'll pay her double."

"Alright, whatever you say. Now on the other side of the house, The Foster-Mays group are waiting for your sign-off on their IPO papers. Mrs. Bianchi called and she thinks her husband knows about the blind trust you set up. And that sexy ass Mr. Liek of Melanin Construction wants you in New York. He has another investment he'd like to discuss with you. You also have two—possibly three—new clients that I'm vetting. One owns a marijuana dispensary chain in Colorado."

"Set up a meeting with Bianchi, bring me the IPO papers and let me know when you've completed the vetting."

"One more thing... well, actually two. *Philadelphia Magazine* would like to interview you for a spread, and *The Daily News* is hoping to feature you in their 'Sexy Singles' issue."

"You already know the answer is no to both of those requests. Now do me a favor, give me an hour and close the door."

"You got it!"

For over an hour, I contemplate the fact that Ms. Cosby has me by the balls in a high-stakes game that I can't afford to lose. Canceling the deal with her daughter isn't an option... I'd be leaving too much money on the table. There has to be a way around all this. I just have to find it.

Chapter Four

The Goodman Firm

Our new offices at Liberty Place have cemented The Goodman Firm as a top-tier brokerage house, providing personalized services for high-net-worth investors. With our four full-time employees, we boast 70 percent investment clients and 30 percent ticket concierge business, which I rarely touch anymore. What others don't know, is that my privately held real estate business, Maddox Investments, is also run out of this office and handled solely between me, my accountant and my lawyer.

It's been over a week since we've moved into the office and I've yet to work in the space. Part of that is my own paranoia that Ms. Turner-Cosby might have my office bugged. It doesn't help that when I walk in there this afternoon, a frenzied Shanté is giving directions to florists, caterers and whoever else her and my mother have hired for the occasion. Since I'm not in the mood for hosting a party, I bypass most of it and slip into my office until there's a knock on the door.

"Son, why are you still in here working?"

"Look at you! Who you trying to catch tonight?" I joke, looking at my mother all dolled up in a royal blue dress accenting her short, silver hair.

Embarrassed, she smooth's her dress down and says, "Son, I'm too old to be catching anything. Now c'mon your guests are arriving! Put this stuff away."

"You know I don't like all this attention."

"Assuming you like the way your bank accounts are growing, I suggest you get out there and land this firm some new clients."

Since my mother is usually right, I roll back my chair, stand up, kiss her on the cheek and reply, "Whatever you say, mother."

The reception area and conference room are filled with clients from both sides of the house, along with former colleagues, local politicians and partners from the banking community. Among them are Thomas Blake, my attorney, and Lisette Trombetta, the forensic accountant who oversees my finances. I've already spoken to them about the possibility of cashing out in case Ms. Turner-Cosby follows through on her threat.

Unbeknownst to our esteemed guests, Hampton has inserted the right balance of available men and women as props to fulfill clients' off-the-book needs, giving credence to my late father's advice of always staying close to the resources other people want. The other rule he'd given me of not shitting where you eat, well, I've already broken that one with Tiffany.

In the midst of offering advice to Grant McNally, a hedge fund manager from Chicago, I begin to notice guests speaking in hushed tones as they make a path for whoever has stepped off the elevator. Assuming that Hampton has invited some athlete or other celebrity friend, I pay no attention until he saunters up behind me.

"Man, you didn't tell me *she* was coming. How'd you pull that shit off?"

Giving me a congratulatory patting on the back, Grant says, "If *she's* in, I'm in."

"Who's in?" I ask, turning around to realize they are referring to an uninvited Raquel Turner-Cosby who is commanding the attention of the entire room.

My body stiffens. Had she found out about the night I'd spent with her daughter? Had they set me up and she's come here to expose me?

"Damn, what you do to get her here? I didn't even know she was out the joint yet," comments my friend Miguel, who's walked over to stand between Hampton and me.

"The way I see it, your billion dollars just walked through the door," confirms Hampton.

The three of us watch as this woman easily engages in conversation and takes pictures with each person who greets and welcomes her home. She carries the room, emanating power and elite social status, and causing an excitement among people who are wealthy, but none of whom can be considered billionaires like her.

She again wears black, this time a low-waist dress with pleats at the bottom and black heels with gold-tipped toes. Her salon-tanned skin and layered blond-and-gray hair is perfectly swept to one side, and held back with a diamond clip. She carries no purse, and the only jewelry she wears is a pair of diamond studs that really are large enough to choke a mule.

Not having known her before she went to federal prison, I would be content just to observe her move through the crowd, until I see her walk over to greet my mother. That is a personal threat, making me regret that I hadn't shot her that night in my office. Hastening my steps through the conference room and out to the reception area, I step in between them.

"Ms. Turner-Cosby, thank you for coming," I lie, reaching out to shake her hand.

"Mr. Goodman, what a beautiful space." She leans in to kiss my cheek, "Please, I've told you before, call me Raquel."

I see cell phones rising to take our picture along with the contracted photographer. All of which I'm sure will end up on social media and beyond.

"Son, I was telling Raquel that we had to beg you to leave that storefront."

Why is my mother already on a first name basis with her?

"Mrs. Goodman, your son is a smart businessman, that's why I've insisted he manage my funds," she lies, loud enough for others to hear.

"Yes, he is, and I'm so proud of him," my mother exclaims, squeezing my forearm.

"Mom, can you give us a minute please?"

"Sure. And Raquel, I'm looking forward to afternoon tea at Lacroix."

What the hell is she talking about? There is no way I'm letting my mother spend time alone with this woman. Lacing my arm through hers, I guide her away from the crowd and down the hall towards my office, closing the door behind us.

As if we are sparring partners, she stands against the windows and I take position against the closed door, anticipating her next move.

"What the fuck are you doing here?"

With her arms folded across her chest, she looks me over from my shoes to my sport coat.

"I'm sure you realize the impact my presence has made here tonight."

She couldn't be more exact in her statement. I am positive Hampton is already in the conference room using her as leverage among our guests. Unfortunately, he has no idea how high the stakes are.

"Like I said, what the fuck are you doing here?"

"I have an opportunity for you, as well as my daughter, and I'd like you to convince her to invest."

"Do it yourself. I've decided to rescind my agreement with your daughter."

She steps towards me and for a moment I imagine myself pushing her through the glass window of my 14th floor office.

"You won't do that, not unless you want your voyeuristic habits exposed. Not only would your business not survive that but your mother... it would kill her."

She's right. The public embarrassment for my mother will be insufferable. Also, if she leaks that video, the SEC, IRS and possibly even the Feds will investigate me, to say nothing about the civil lawsuits from restaurants and patrons who may feel violated.

Rather than take that chance, for now, I choose to listen.

Chapter Five

Divine Lorraine

My first official appointment with Tiffany comes a month after our encounter. Her assistant had called my office to schedule an 8:15 a.m. meeting at the governor's Philadelphia residence located inside the historic Divine Lorraine building at Broad and Fairmount.

Upon presenting myself to the concierge, I'm directed to unit 1447, where a state police officer standing outside greets me then steps aside so I can ring the bell to the apartment.

To my surprise when the door opens, I find myself standing eye-to-eye with Pennsylvania's first African-American Governor, Malik D. Skinner. His wife stands next to him, her arm laced through his. He reaches out to grip my hand in a firm shake.

"Good morning, Mr. Goodman. I see my wife has you up early."

"Good morning, Governor... Mrs. Skinner."

"It's my understanding you have a solid reputation in this city. It would be great to have a sit-down with you."

"Be an honor, Sir," I respond, knowing I have not one good reason to sit down with this man.

He turns from me, kisses his wife on lips painted pale pink and says to her, "I'll see you and the kids back in Harrisburg this evening."

"In time for dinner?"

"Affirmative," he answers before affectionately pecking her again on the lips.

After he leaves, I give Tiffany a once-over. She is wearing an ankle-length, peach-colored dress, fastened with six pearl buttons down the front and a pink leather belt pinched at her waist. On her feet, she wears flat-jeweled sandals, exposing pale pink toenails, which I now recall having had in my mouth.

"Bryce, I'll be just a moment. Please help yourself," she says gesturing towards the dining room with matching pale pink fingernails.

The apartment is one of the larger units in the building, sparsely yet richly appointed; making it obvious it isn't their permanent residence. There are pictures of their two children, one of her and the governor on a beach, and a picture with people the public knows to be her adoptive parents, along with her sister the restaurateur and her brother the MLB All-Star.

On the dining room buffet, there is an untouched spread of fruit, pastries, coffee, juice and a glass pitcher filled with water and floating cucumber slices. I wonder if she's expecting someone else to join us.

Since I am neither thirsty nor hungry, I take a seat at the table, from where I observe her dress; fluttering in and out with each step she takes across the room to retrieve her laptop from the coffee table. Under all that pink there is a set of legs that I recently had wrapped around my shoulders.

Tiffany seats herself at the head of the table. When she opens her laptop, I catch the stray scent of her fragrance. To maintain my focus, I open my iPad and direct my attention to TJS Holdings.

To begin our meeting, I share the risks she can take with her current investments and areas that will offer growth to her portfolio, including the expansion of her charities.

"That sounds reasonable. I'd also like 5K a month directed to the Johnson Family Trust and another 5K quarterly deposited into my nephew's blind trust."

While her fingers mindlessly caress the keyboard of her laptop, she continues. "Essentially, I want to see growth and I don't want to wait long for it."

Every time she speaks, her demeanor is so businesslike that I can't imagine ever having had sex with the woman. But the telltale signs are there, especially the way her almond-shaped eyes barely meet mine and the way she keeps checking her nails, as if she would even allow one to be chipped.

"To be effective," I start, "I'd like us to build a long-term relationship, centered on a foundation of trust, which you should know is my top priority. I also need to understand the amount of risk you're comfortable with."

"I've already proven that I'm willing to take risks," she responds. "How often should I expect to meet with you?"

Knowing she is referring to her visit to my apartment, I simply nod. "Clients hear from me daily with any changes to their accounts."

Leaning forward, with her hand resting on the side of her face she says, "That's fair enough. Now what can you tell me about 'The Giving Pledge'?"

"It's where billionaires commit to donating more than half of their *known* wealth to philanthropic causes or charities. Is that what you're interested in doing?" I reply liking the fact that she seems to know what money can do and that by giving it away, she can triple her wealth.

Attentively she listens, as I go on to tell her what is involved and how she might go about making a pledge.

Interrupting me, she asks, "Excuse me, Bryce, are you thirsty?"

She stands and goes over to the buffet to pour us both a glass of water. I watch through the mirror at her reflection glancing back at me.

"Is the governor aware of your net worth and how it might impact his financial disclosure?" I ask.

Judging by the numbers in her portfolio, I doubt that the governor or his constituents are aware that their First Lady has a net worth of 25.1 million. Her mother Ms. Turner-Cosby, on the other hand, as the previous Chairman and CEO of privately held RTC Holdings, is worth over 10 billion.

Before answering my question, she returns to her seat and crosses her legs, exposing her ankles and calves. Imagining the heat lying between those thighs, I am now thirsty for that glass of water.

"He's aware of what's appropriate for his position. Anything else is confidential and my lawyers have instructed me to keep it that way." She uncrosses her legs.

"Is there a pre-nup?" I ask, unable to take my eyes away from her throat as she swallows.

"Originally there was no need, but as things have changed in the last few years, the appropriate papers have been signed," she responds, patting the soft bun at the nape of her neck as if it were out of place. Nothing about her is out of place. She is perfect.

"We should discuss Raquel. From the pictures in the media of your open house, it's obvious you're aware that she's been released. As you can see, we have quite a few shared investments, so you can be certain she'll try to manipulate you in an effort to determine where and how I'm investing. It would be best if you notify me before speaking with her."

As she speaks, all I hear are the demands she'd made on me at my apartment: *"Let me ride it...I wanna taste it...wait...wait."*

"Your interests are my priority," I respond without telling her that Ms. Cosby has also managed to retain my services. A conflict of interest I'm sure, but everything about these two is conflicting. I wonder how she'll react if I tell her that her mother is blackmailing me. Either way I can't risk it, not yet.

By 10:00 a.m. our work is complete and I'm anxious to get the hell out of there. I close my iPad, push back from the table and stand up to leave.

"I think we're good."

"Are we clear on my expectations?"

"Yes ma'am."

"Might I suggest you keep your door locked?"

"About that..."

"What about it? You had a service I required and..." she pauses to run the tip of her tongue across her top, then bottom lip, "...I trusted you could be effective and we both came away satisfied."

My phone vibrates with a prearranged text from Shanté in case I needed an excuse to exit. I don't even bother to take it out my pocket.

"Tiffany, if we could take a moment, I'd like to apologize for whatever transpired when you came to my apartment."

"There's certainly no need to apologize. You gave me exactly... well, I should say *more* than I expected."

"I'm sorry about that. I'm not a drinking man and it wasn't a particularly good night," I admit to her, never having apologized to anyone this much in my life, especially when it comes to how I handle a woman during sex.

She rears back in her chair, and with her eyes steady on me she adds, "He doesn't like it when you leave marks."

"What? What marks? Who doesn't like it?"

She smiles for the first time all morning, "The Governor and I have an open marriage."

"SHIT! What marks did I leave? Did I hurt you? What did you tell him?"

Standing behind her chair, her breasts are pushing forward making me not only uncomfortable, but I have to inconspicuously shift my swelling dick.

"He thinks I have a female lover. It's better that way."

"Do you? Have one?"

She removes a joint from the buffet drawer and lights it.

"When I'm in the mood, I have what I want."

"Tiffany, I apologize, but you did leave something behind that night. *Your shoe?*"

"Toss it. Here, this belongs to you," she says, handing me my missing Hublot.

This bitch is crazy.

"I need to go. I have a client waiting at my office."

As I make my way down the hall towards the door I hear her inhale then exhale the joint she's smoking. Not only is this woman a threat to my livelihood, it's clear she's becoming a challenge to my manhood. Yet, I'm intrigued.

"You called me a 'nasty bitch.' The Governor has never called me that."

I try to keep walking but either my feet won't move or my dick is too hard.

"Tiffany, I have to go. You'll hear from me by Wednesday with recommendations." Shit, today is Wednesday. "I mean by Friday."

"It was the slapping of your dick back and forth across my face that gave me the bruises."

Without turning around, I hear the heels of her sandals stepping towards me. Her arms encircle my waist and she yanks the tail of my shirt out of the front of my pants. I tell myself to move, to get the fuck out of there, yet I don't take one step. Nuzzling her head against my back, I hear her breathing in my scent. Perhaps I've judged wrong, because at this moment Tiffany appears more dangerous than her mother.

Her hands reach down to grope my dick through my pants and she says, "I keep remembering that sweet musky scent down around your balls."

I'd obviously been right. She is a nasty bitch. But is she brazen enough to fuck me in the home she shares with her husband? I turn around to face her, hoping I can convince her this isn't a good idea.

"You don't wanna do this again," I beg of the woman who has already settled down onto her knees and is unzipping my pants.

Closing her eyes, she curls her soft hands around my dick, applying a light pressure as she strokes, releases, then tightens her grip.

33

She kisses the head.

"I been thinking about this dick, how thick it is," stroking it from base to tip, "this fat head."

She strokes it again.

"The way it sits up and points at me."

She flicks her tongue at it.

"And all these veins that run around it, m-m-m-m."

She traces them with her tongue.

Looking down at her, I watch as she draws in a deep breath, and opens her mouth, allowing the head of my dick to ease past her tongue and into the back of her throat.

My dick nestles there for a moment, then with a precise sucking motion, it begins to dip and recede, making the governor's wife if not the most gifted woman to ever suck my dick, then certainly the wealthiest.

I try not to, but I groan when the heat and wetness of her mouth closes totally around my throbbing dick. To ensure she gets it all, she holds onto the back of my thighs, her nails digging in, pulling me closer.

I give in, rise up on my toes and, with my hands pressing down on her head, begin riding in and out of her sweet mouth, my dick brushing against the ridges at the top, its head rolling around inside her jaws. There isn't an inch of her mouth that isn't filled with my dick.

She pulls back and says, "I can taste it, give it to me."

I want to give it to her, shoot my nut in her mouth, all over her face but I'm not going to let her get off that easy—I want her guts.

I push her away and her eyelids flutter open. Bringing her up to her feet, my hands hold onto her face and I kiss her hard, my tongue tearing into her mouth, biting her lips. My hands fight with her clothes.

I lead her by the hand down the hall and back into the dining room. Not wanting to waste time with her buttons, I yank them apart and watch them pop across the room. She'll have to deal with finding them later.

The sun shining against her dark and well-cared-for skin is mesmerizing. She goes to step out of her pink G-string but I stop her and say, "Leave them on."

Confident that she has me in her spell, she unsnaps her bra. I push her head back and bite circles around her neck and down to the pure, chocolate mounds of flesh on her chest. As my face gets lost between them, her head falls back and she cries out, "Bryce, don't tease me. I need this."

"You keep saying my name like that and I'm gonna fuck the shit outta you."

She doesn't know that after I finish having my way with her, she'll be no good to the governor or any other lover.

I position her in a chair with her legs up so I can see pink flesh separated by the wet string of her panties. Getting down on my knees, I separate the lips of her pussy with my thumbs and begin lapping at the soft folds of tissue to ensure no juices escape me. She holds onto my head, pushing her pelvis against my face, smothering me with a creamy orgasm.

"Wait, wait," she protests, pushing against my chest, "slow down, I'm not ready."

That's the problem with women, they beg for it and then they want you to wait. Well, waiting isn't one of my strong points.

I slow down, wait for her to regain herself then tell her, "Get up."

Tiffany stands and faces the mirror. I press my dick against her back, reach around and drag my middle finger from her asshole to the top of her clit.

She tries to back away but I hold onto her with both arms as I push two, then three fingers up into her until she surrenders with the splashing of another orgasm into the palm of my hand.

Through the mirror, our eyes lock, giving me confidence that this woman has the perfect amount of skills to receive the beast in me.

Holding onto her hips, I spread her legs apart with my knee and bend her over the buffet. My dick finds its own way inside her. Once I have her open, I thrust into her long and deep, until we gather up a rhythm that goes from slow to fast then slow enough for her to tighten her muscles, so my dick slides out to the very tip, only for her to grind down and take it all back in. I grip the bun on the back of her head and hold her down, pounding into her, as she lies splayed across the buffet. I lift my hips, which allows me to push my dick up into her cervix where her pussy molds and sucks it into a perfect socket.

"This why you called me over here, ain't it?" I say though gritted teeth.

"I can't stop coming...a-h-h-h...don't stop. Come, come with me," she begs, and we don't, not even when her face lands in the tray of neatly cut melons, nor when the pitcher of water crashes to the floor. I don't stop, because I can't.

She attempts to talk, to tell me how good it was. She screams but I realize that it isn't her that's screaming, it's me, calling out her name while squirting a nut so hard I fear I might pass out. Holding onto her around the waist, I fall back into the chair and she follows, collapsing into my lap.

Chapter Six

Living for the City

The ability to go unnoticed in Philly no longer exists. Ms. Turner-Cosby's visit to my open house made certain of that. In an attempt to clear my head and line up whatever move might be next, I hop on an Acela to New York.

The first of three meetings is in the Diamond District with Daniel Abendum, a jeweler who'd entrusted his finances to me when I first opened shop. For inheritance tax purposes, Mr. Abendum, whose health is failing, needs to relinquish his business to his son. I've cautioned him against it, since junior has more interest in becoming a film director than a jeweler.

Sitting in his second floor office, over a breakfast tray filled with bagels and smoked salmon, he carefully explains to me the Jewish tradition of a man's firstborn son inheriting the family business. I, in turn, explain to him, that in order to save his fortune he needs to tear up his will and put his 13.3 million in an irrevocable trust with his daughter as the main trustee, who will then be able to distribute his assets according to his directive. If not, I tell him, it will be tied up in probate and he'll suffer a substantial loss. At the idea of losing any portion of what he's worked for, he agrees to the new terms.

Before heading to my next meeting, I ask my driver to take me to Fifth Avenue to pick up birthday presents for Shanté. My assistant loves everything Gucci, and even with the generous salary we pay her, she refuses to pay full price so she always settles for knock-offs. The sales clerk at Gucci convinces me to purchase the Supreme Tote. I know Shanté will be pleased.

Next, I stop at the Apple store to pick up a MacBook Pro then have it all shipped to our office where my mother is planning on hosting a small celebration for Shanté's 27th birthday.

The afternoon's final destination is the West Village for a celebratory lunch with my partners, Jason Rutley and Guy Weilheimer of TixMixx in the private cellar at The Left Bank. Two years ago, we'd begun the process of launching an online ticket business, and already we find ourselves competing for a share of the market with their former employers at StubHub and Ticketmaster.

By the time I arrive, in addition to my partners and their wives, there is a group of about 30 people assembled in the room, most of whom are our hungry millennial employees. Once I finish talking with everyone and give the obligatory toasts, I am ready to dig into the trays of food that have been placed on our table.

Two hours later, I go upstairs to leave when my eyes catch sight of a woman making her way from the main dining room to the ladies room. My anxieties rise, it's been months since I've watched unsuspecting women. I hesitate taking the risk in Philly, especially since Ms. Turner-Cosby entered my life, but this afternoon I'm in New York.

With slight trepidation, I slip inside the bathroom. The stall next to the one she occupies is open, and as usual, the gap between the stalls is wide enough for me to get a slanted view of the woman. Her back is to me as she plops down, crushing the paper seat cover, and I hear her let out an exasperating breath as she pees. The black skirt she wears is hiked up to her waist, and beige Spanx stretch across her ankles. Stepping out of what are probably 3-inch heels, she rests her plump little feet on the cold tiles.

On her head, to restrain a full and bouncy Afro, she sports a multi-colored headband. Her ears are adorned with silver studs, and around her neck she wears a black choker with silver amulets. Multi-colored beaded bracelets decorate her left wrist.

Upon finishing her business, she pats herself dry, but instead of getting up, she sits there massaging her temples. She steps back into her shoes; the sexiness of her thick calves is exquisite. She exits the stall and stands over the sink. Her reflection in the mirror is of a woman with sunburnt skin and bountiful breasts that appear to be fighting against the front of her white, button-down shirt. She looks to be in her mid-30s with an anguished look on her face. What's wrong with her? Who has she dined with?

She washes her hands, checks under her unpolished nails, and then applies some moisturizer. After sending a text on her phone, she removes lip-gloss from her tote bag and reapplies a shade of red that makes her look like a child playing in her mother's makeup. Then she's gone.

Back in my room at the Gansevoort I set my alarm for midnight but it wasn't necessary. I awake at 10:30 with a call from Raquel Turner-Cosby.

"Bryce here."

"How are things going with my daughter?"

"I assume she's satisfied. Why are you asking?"

"And the meeting at her residence... how did that go?"

"Listen, I'm not sure what your play is here but my principles won't allow me to disclose information about your daughter's investments."

"I can appreciate your candor, Mr. Goodman. With that aside, upon returning to your office, you'll have the outline of the joint venture I mentioned. It's your job to convince her to sign on as a silent partner. Are we clear?"

"Goodnight."

* * *

As with all my clients, regardless of their profession, I take a pledge of discretion. It's even more important for Liek Mills. As the proprietor of Melanin Construction, he isn't my typical investment client but he fit in the category of two dope slingers to whom I provide services. I've infused their cash into investments that have legitimized their assets and given them a substantial retirement fund. Others might call it money laundering, but with a net worth of 70 million, Liek's money deserves to be handled with respect.

Approaching his ridiculously priced, bulletproof Bentley Bentayga Mulliner, I expect to hear loud music. When the door opens, it's surprisingly quiet. Two bodyguards sit in the front seat, with Liek in the back. We are encased between two soundproof panels.

"What's up brother? How you been?" he asks as we shake hands and embrace.

"Liek, I'm good. How 'bout you?"

"Bry, long as I'm on this side of the dirt, I'm solid. You ready for a night out?"

"Yea man, you know I love this city," I reply, unsure of what a night out with him consists of.

"You 'bout to get a real taste of it. Plus I got someone with skills you ain't never seen and I'm gone need you to look out for her."

"The Goodman Firm doesn't represent celebrities, you know that, right? They're too much trouble."

"I guess that's a compliment to brothers in my line of business."

"It is, my friend. Clients like yourself make a decision and stick with it. Celebrities are too indecisive and in no way am I a 'yes' man," I exclaim, when in fact that's exactly the role Ms. Turner-Cosby expects me to play.

"I know, I know. She ain't a celebrity yet but she will be, and she'll make us both a ton of cash."

The idea of dealing with a female seeking stardom is of no interest to me but there's no harm in an introduction. Worse case I can turn her over to Hampton who's been after me to at least add athletes to our roster.

As we glide through the streets of New York, Liek points out the properties he owns which, in Manhattan alone, consist of six, four-level parking garages, a nightclub in Tribeca and two bodegas. In between, he fields calls, as would any CEO, except it is after one in the morning and they aren't international. Meanwhile, out of a crystal flute, I sip on Dom Perignon from the chilling ring between us.

"Here's what I need your assistance with. I wanna go legit, no bullshit. I got 7 mill I'm reinvesting. It'll bring back 20 then I'm done. I've already sold off parts of the business, the rest I'm turning over to my lieutenant. I'm tired of these streets. Shit is different now. You know me, regardless of my profession I'm a fair man and these brothers been loyal to me."

Liek was right he didn't give handouts and has rightfully employed people inside and outside of his organization, investing in opportunities that give jobs to his community. At my advice, he'd established a nonprofit but he's also impervious to the rules of the establishment. Under better circumstances, with his business acumen he could work on Wall Street. Isn't that always the case?

"What I'm hearing is, you want to take an early retirement and you'd like me to see how best to reinvest your retirement fund without any penalties or losses and at the lowest tax rate?" I say, all the while wishing that were an option for me. How could it be when I'm shaped and tied to Philly?

"I mean I'm still gonna get some monthly dividends but yeah, I wanna retire. Can you move—I mean re-invest—the 20 for me when it comes back around? Shouldn't take long."

"Usual fee?"

"And a bonus."

"I should be able to pull it off but I'll need at least two months to figure out which accounts to run it through," I say. In actuality, washing 20 million dollars will take a lot of creativity. If successful, it will get me closer to my financial goal.

"See, that's the shit I'm talking 'bout."

"But Liek, I gotta ask, isn't getting out the game the most dangerous time?"

Nodding toward the front seat he says, "These niggas got me covered like the secret service and will take out any muthafucka coming at me. If some shit do go down, you don't wanna know where those bodies buried."

"Shit, I got a body I'd like to bury."

"Bry, I ain't ever heard you talk like that! But if you got a nigga fuckin wit' you, shit, I don't give a fuck if it's one of them crazy bitches, I'll send the brothas down to Philly tonight. All you gotta do is say the word."

Considering his offer to make my problem disappear, without it tracing back to me is tempting, but what would it mean? It would mean that with Ms. Cosby buried, Tiffany would be the heir to all her mother's assets, thereby benefitting me.

"I'm gonna tuck that in and get back to you."

As he takes another call, we pull into a gated Brooklyn warehouse. After scanning the parking lot packed with high-end luxury vehicles, I know this is far from your trap nightclub.

"This one of yours?"

"It's a private spot I set up for folks who like to party without any eyes on 'em."

A curbside attendant opens our door. As I approach the entryway, I take note of a sign in chrome letters that reads "10X." Once inside, a male and female concierge both escort us down a winding hallway that opens up into an expansive and exceptionally well-decorated room. If there are celebrities present, I can't tell. It feels uniquely private.

Proud of his venue, Liek takes the time to describe every piece of furniture he has personally selected with his designer. Around the exterior of the room are booths of white marble, upholstered in herringbone reds and nickel. Crystal chandeliers hang from the ceiling and on the walls are floating mirrors and crystal sconces. The room-length bar has a centerpiece tower of the Manhattan skyline and is bookended by 72-inch flat screens. The audio and video systems are state-of-the-art and Liek confirms that the cost was well above 1 million.

We take seats with a group of ten of Liek's closest friends and family at an 8-foot solid walnut and bronze Knight Table that he says cost him 70K. It's his most prized piece, designed by someone named Barlas Baylor. According to Liek, Beyoncé and Jay-Z own the only other one of its kind.

We barely finish introductions when two servers place bottles of Grey Goose VX, Hennessy Privilege and Macallan M on the table. After my experience drinking that shit, I keep it simple with a Heineken but that doesn't last long because Liek starts to propose a toast with a cart of Ace of Spades Champagne that has been rolled out for the occasion.

After motioning for everyone to stand up, Liek gives a short but solid toast with the group listening to his every word, as the funky beat of Vince Staples starts rapping "Street Punks" through his million dollar speakers.

"Y'all remember when we was young boys slinging on the corner? We idolized guys like Nino Brown, Frank Lucas, Tony Montana, and even though Tony ain't like us mullions, we watched the Sopranos too. But that shit gave us an advantage. We peeped their mistakes, how they fucked up and that shit kept us from stepping in the same shit."

I hold my glass in the air and listen and I realize I'm no different than Liek. Where I'd idolized those who'd attained financial success on Wall Street—my father among them—he'd done the same with his idolization of men of power, wealth, and those who had the respect as an organized crime boss.

I'm caught off-guard when Liek puts his arm around me and continues with, "Now this brother right here, for the last five years he's been my consigliore which is why we now have the opportunity to live like legitimate kings. Because of this man, we ain't just giving out turkeys at Thanksgiving and toys at Christmas, we providing jobs and making sure our people get the proper healthcare. Shit, he even made sure a brother like me can retire... respectfully."

"Whether you been my day one or came on board later, y'all ain't never let me down and I hope I ain't let you down. Cause you know my motto, if I got it—" they chime in and everyone says together, "You got it."

"To my family."

After the toast, folks gather to take pictures to post on social media. I offer to take the shots on their cameras. I've seen the same movies they have, and I know pictures always come back to haunt folks when the FEDS and DEA showed up.

While we were toasting, Liek had ordered every item on a menu that I hadn't even seen. Platters of food are brought out, making the table look like a spread from the centerfold of *Food and Wine*. I'm impressed.

We take our seats and I help myself to some roasted chicken, lobster bisque and a puff pastry topped with chanterelle mushrooms. Each bite melts in my mouth and my taste buds explode with the flavors from an unexpected blend of seasonings. I glance down the table and see all the women taking pictures of their food and the bottles of champagne. I try not to watch as the brother across from me ruins his crab-stuffed filet mignon by drowning it in A1 sauce. There isn't one person among our group who isn't enjoying this meal.

I've eaten at Michelin-star restaurants on the East and West coasts but this place is truly a hidden gem. I'm curious to know who the chef is behind it all.

"Liek, who the hell do you have in the kitchen?"

Sucking a bone from his cherry-glazed ribs clean, he responds, "I knew you were gonna like this shit. Here she come now."

The chef emerges from the kitchen and it's clear she's the celebrity at 10X—for good reason. She stops at each alcove and table, greeting people who are applauding her talent in the kitchen. Some even pass her envelopes, which makes me wish I too had one for her.

As she approaches our table, I notice she has plenty of meat on her bones to fit her profession, a reflection that she enjoys her own cooking. She wears a white coat and pants, Dansko shoes and instead of a Chef's hat; she's covered her head with a thin white silk scarf pulled an inch past her hairline. Most men might consider her average, maybe even overweight, but I'm not most men. I believe all women are beautiful, they just don't believe it themselves.

"Chef Z, this here is my man Bryce I been telling you about."

I stand to shake her hand and wait until she slips into the seat across from me next to Liek before I sit back down. There's something strikingly familiar about her I just can't place... then I notice the choker around her neck. She's the woman from the ladies room at The Left Bank. But this woman doesn't appear anguished; and gone are the high-heel shoes and ill-fitting clothes. She is obviously in her element.

"Nice to meet you, Bryce," she says, smiling from a mouth that gleams with perfect white teeth and eyes that hold fake lashes.

"My pleasure, Chef. Your food...it's exceptional, the flavorings. I can't get enough."

"Thank you. It's a 'lil bit a spices I brought from home that I like to play with."

"Home?" I ask, noticing the accent she's trying to hide.

Ignoring my question about home, she asks, "Did Liek tell you I'm opening a culinary school down in your city of brotherly love? Zinzi's Culinary Institute. I understand you're the person I should know."

Not wanting to appear too anxious to get a taste of her, I reply, "It depends on what your needs are."

"We already locked down a location," says Liek, not waiting for Zinzi to answer. "Got a three-story building on North Broad, near Temple and the work is just about done."

"There's only space for 100 students but we've a waiting list of 330 and between 10X, the school and my private clients, I'm back and forth twice a week on Amtrak," Zinzi chimes in.

My eyes follow as she speaks with her hands, knowing they've prepared the food I've eaten. I want to taste them, lick the tips of each polish-free finger to see if that's where she keeps the flavors.

"And where are you staying?"

"Marriott on Market Street for now. Liek rented me an apartment at some place called the *Lorraine* but I've yet to see it."

"Divine Lorraine," I repeat, remembering that Tiffany has a place in the same building, which can't be more of a damn conflict.

"The goal for me and my staff is to educate underprivileged children on how to be chefs, you know develop their basic skills around the kitchen, then develop real culinary skills that are marketable."

"Will it also serve as a restaurant? I mean it could help to offset your costs, possibly be a basis for scholarships." I glance at Liek, who is clearly her benefactor and add, "It would also mean a bit more construction. Maybe even consider some non-profit options."

Liek, picking up the cues I'm laying down about using the construction of the restaurant to run his money through, gives a slow nod of the head in acknowledging that his choice in choosing me was right all along.

"You hear that shit? Z, I told you to stop meeting with those weak-ass Wall Street boys and let my man handle your shit. That's what we'll do. Bry, you can set it all up right?"

I now know why she'd appeared bewildered in the ladies room. "When do you plan to open?"

"September 26 the first class starts. I'm moving down there next week."

"I'm sure I can have a few options ready for you by then."

A smile plays at the corner of her lips. "I guess Liek was right, he said you were the money man."

"I do my best."

She slides back her chair and stands up. "I'm glad you enjoyed your meal. Dessert is on its way. It's an apple and pomegranate cobbler with homemade ice cream. Liek loves it."

"I'm sure I will too," I reply, realizing that if Zinzi is one of Liek's women, I'm in trouble.

Chapter Seven

Mommy Dearest

Looming in front of me is a 3:00 p.m. meeting with Tiffany and Ms. Turner-Cosby, who is seeking her daughters inclusion as a silent partner in the purchase of the Carolina Panthers football team. The deal has received approval from the NFL, as well as Ms. Turner-Cosby's board of directors at RTC Holdings, and will be her first major acquisition since her release from federal prison. The Goodman Firm is set up as only minor players—a conduit to convince Tiffany to be in business with her mother, rather than simply a moneymaker. Now that I understand our role, this arrangement will work as long as Ms. Turner-Cosby doesn't find out I'm fucking her daughter.

With the assistance of a private investigator, I've discovered it is indeed public knowledge that Tiffany and her siblings were adopted by an African-American couple who live in Moorestown, NJ. Her siblings had sought out and found their biological parents but Tiffany has always been outspoken about having no interest in going down that path. What isn't public knowledge is that Ms. Turner-Cosby is her biological mother and a West Indian man named Firoz Alleyne is her father.

Ms. Turner-Cosby had been a 15-year-old girl who's blue blood, Main Line family had insisted she put her newborn bi-racial child up for adoption. For the purposes of this business deal I thought it best to entrust these details to a very surprised Hampton.

In preparation for the meeting, we closed our offices at noon to ensure no other clients are present. Since my partner is the best at assessing risk and finding the loophole in any kind of deal, I rely on his diligence to run the numbers. It pays off, as Hampton found the perfect loophole to insert The Goodman Firm not only as their broker, but also as a minority partner under TJS Holdings.

Ms. Turner-Cosby is the first to arrive, with her daughter walking in directly behind her, both of them hiding behind black sunglasses. When Shanté escorts them into the conference room it's obvious they have the same walk, leading with their looks; heads up, shoulders back and hips that deliver a slight swivel.

Ms. Turner-Cosby wears a black and gray jacquard print dress with three-quarter length sleeves, topped off with a pair of pearl earrings sculpted in gold. Two strands of pearls encircle her neck and her hair is dyed and trimmed to perfection. My eyes hover over Tiffany, who's fitted herself into a bottle-green dress, paired with a cropped double-breasted black blazer. On her ears are small figure eight diamond earrings that sparkle in the sunlight streaming through the conference room windows. These women may be in complete contrast as far as skin color, but they're both conservative in their appearance and demeanor. To avoid eye contact with each other, they sit side-by-side, leaving an empty seat between them.

I complete the initial pleasantries of introducing them to my partner and then open the meeting by restating the highlights of the deal, paying particular attention to the benefits to Tiffany's portfolio. I then turn the floor over to Hampton who drills down through the details, allowing for, and subsequently fielding, questions. None of this is new to Ms. Turner-Cosby, she's been through these types of acquisitions numerous times. But it is new to Tiffany.

The collective mood in the room is more of anxiety then tension, as Ms. Turner-Cosby absentmindedly fingers the pearls at her neck and Tiffany caresses the rim of her water glass with her fingertips without ever taking a sip.

Tiffany expresses concern about the vulnerability of exposure, not only as a team owner but also as the secret daughter of a white billionaire. She claims it is for the governor's sake, but I know better—she still doesn't want to be personally affiliated with Ms. Cosby even though she's previously accepted public contributions to her charitable platform.

Tiffany fails to avoid eye contact with me, and every time our eyes meet, she shifts her focus to Hampton at the front of the room. Either it's impossible for this woman to rein in her sexuality or maybe it's me who feels certain that I can taste the stickiness between her legs every time she shifts in her seat.

Tiffany signs off on the deal that is structured to give the majority ownership to Ms. Turner-Cosby and herself 20 percent, from which The Goodman Firm takes 2 percent in case the need ever arises for another public fronting owner. I have a bottle of champagne on standby but neither seems to be in a celebratory mood.

Tiffany is the first to push back from the table, exchanging an awkward goodbye with her mother. She asks me to walk her out. Meanwhile, Ms. Turner-Cosby lingers behind, engaging in further conversation with Hampton.

"Thanks for agreeing to meet here today," I say to her back as she pushes the button for the elevator. "I'm sure you'll find the deal profitable."

Abruptly she turns to face me, her body so close I can smell her breath.

"I don't know much about the finances behind football so I guess I'm forced to rely on and trust *you*."

Positive that Shanté is listening from where she sits perched at the reception desk, I lower my voice, "I value your trust but it's her you hate."

"I don't hate her."

"Then what is it?"

Even as she slips her sunglasses onto her face, a hint of tears glisten in her eyes.

"What she hasn't told you is that I visited her in Danbury, where she was still unable to explain why she abandoned her only child, yet allowed us to live in the same city. And now she expects to have a relationship with me *and* my children."

"I doubt the decision was hers to make. I mean, you have to admit, being part of her bloodline has benefitted you *and your family*."

"Seems to me you're benefitting the most," she answers, before backing into the elevator.

"I didn't ask for your business or hers."

"Yet I don't see you turning down our business or anything else that's been offered to you."

To the closing elevator doors I reply, "Good day, Tiffany."

Where I originally thought they might be polar opposites, there is no doubt in my mind that when necessary, Tiffany can be as ruthless as her mother.

As soon as I turn around, Shanté offers up some unsolicited advice.

"Boss, I don't mean to ear hustle but don't let that boujee-ass woman get you all fucked up. Just 'cause she got money don't mean she ain't got issues. I don't care if she is the governor's wife."

"Shanté, women would be boring if they didn't have issues."

"I'm just saying, she thirsty. I can see it in her eyes."

When I step back into the conference room, Ms. Turner-Cosby and Hampton are wrapping things up.

"Mr. Goodman do you have time on your schedule to continue our discussion?" Ms. Turner-Cosby asks, all while dismissing Hampton with the cut of her eyes.

"Did we miss something?"

"There's another opportunity I'd like to discuss that might further enrich the Goodman Firm."

"My office okay?"

"I'd prefer this evening, seven o'clock at my home."

Out the corner of my eye I see Shanté shaking her head.

"Not a problem. You're the client."

"I'll have my driver pick you up."

"Not necessary, I can get there on my own."

Back in my office, I read a text from Zinzi, cancelling our dinner for later that evening. She and I had had several conversations mostly centered on her business goals but her text saves me from having to disappoint her, which I've done twice now due to client commitments. Once again, getting to know her personally will have to wait.

After taking a 45-minute conference call with my TixxMixx partners and returning several emails and calls, I have some time to kill before meeting with Ms. Turner-Cosby. I wrap up things on my desk and walk with Hampton over to Del Frisco's to meet our trusted friend, Miguel. It takes us at least 15 minutes to get to the table, as we stop and speak to several colleagues who want to congratulate us on our move and our growing client roster.

"What's up, Miguel? How's business?" I ask, after shaking hands and giving him a quick embrace.

"Pile of sand, man, pile of sand. What about you? Word is you only taking on billion dollar clients. Leaving the crumbs to Hamp," he jokes.

"Let's say I'm reserving my services for the high-cotton investors."

Waiting until the waitress finishes serving our drinks—scotch neat for Hampton and Old Fashioneds for me and Miguel, he continues, "Shit, the cotton don't get no softer than Raquel Turner-Cosby."

Taking a moment to realize the magnitude of who I'm dealing with, even with her lingering threat, I respond, "Unexpected capital, brother, is all I can say."

"That's big time shit, man, congratulations."

Holding up my glass offering a toast, I say, "Thanks goes to Hamp."

"I'm telling you, man, that ol' broad looking for some work. I can see it in her eyes," Hampton declares, insinuating Ms. Turner-Cosby has a personal interest in me.

I'm not listening; instead I have my eyes on three women, two white and one black, who are making their way downstairs to the ladies room. I hate when they go in groups, it makes it harder for me to follow; what's more... watch.

"Get the fuck outta here! That woman is all about her money."

"Hamp, you saying she fell for the fried ice cream?" Miguel jokes.

"Yes! At a high level."

They tap glasses.

"Bryce, we know you like to keep your shit close to the vest when it comes to women but that's some center-cut pussy right there."

"Fuck outta here."

"Seriously, I doubt she looking for a relationship. Women like her just wanna get fucked real decent."

Miguel chimes in. "The way I see it, at least at that level, you don't have to worry about dealing with her jealous friends."

"How many times do I have to reiterate to you brothas that no matter what a woman's socioeconomic level, good dick will always be their weakness?"

Knowing what they both state is true we all laugh and tap glasses again.

"I ain't trying to sleep with that woman and I damn sure don't have time to focus on a relationship," I say. Yet I find myself wondering if Zinzi might be an option. But how can she be when I still don't have a clear picture of her relationship with Liek? To say nothing of how much I enjoy my private time with Tiffany.

"Shit, way I see it all pussy the same...young, old, fat, skinny, from the projects to the penthouse, it's still pussy," says Miguel.

"Naw, brothers, I can verify ain't no two pussies the same."

Miguel and I wait, knowing Hampton, who considers himself an expert on women, is about to lay one of his metaphors on us. He leans across the table in an attempt to whisper but the place is too crowded and noisy.

"I mean, take the clit for example. The variety of clits is just like asses. First of all, you got the fat clit that you can pluck back and forth like a little dick," he states, flicking the air with his fingers.

"Now, the small one you gotta pucker up and suck out its shell. And that long one, the one that damn near reaches her ass, she can probably get off on her own with that muthafucka."

By now, the women at the neighboring table have returned and seeing the way they're snickering, they've clearly overhead Hampton's diatribe on clits. To show we are respectful men, I send a bottle of Krug Champagne to their table. In return, we receive their business cards.

"Man, your ass is crazy. Ain't no clit that long."

"Nigga, you ain't seen but one clit in the last 20 years... shit."

"That's cause I'm faithful."

"Wait, wait, let me tell you my favorite one. It's gotta be that juicy swollen clit, that bitch pushes outside them pretty lips, just waiting to be sucked on and that, my brothas, is a clear indicator of top grade, center-cut pussy. And for you Bryce, that's exactly what you got in the ol' broad."

"Ya'll niggas is crazy. I ain't selling my dick to nobody."

"Don't listen to him, that woman already went to jail for one body. I'd stay away from her," Miguel argues.

Maybe they're both right. If I'm being used by Tiffany and played by Ms. Turner-Cosby, the best thing out the deal are the fat checks The Goodman Firm receives from both of them each month.

Any time I get together with these brothers it makes for a good time. The only thing missing tonight is a Cuban and a piece of that center-cut pussy, which for me is Tiffany. I'm tempted to text her but, realizing it's 6:45, I bid my friends goodnight and head to my last meeting of the day.

Chapter Eight

Golden Ticket

A young man whose name and Italian model-like appearance are the definition of a cliché greets me at the front door of Ms. Cosby's 3rd and Delancey Street home.

"Good evening Mr. Goodman, my name is Dante, Ms. Raquel Turner-Cosby's personal assistant. Please follow me."

"Evening, Dante," I reply, following behind him down a narrow hallway lain with an oriental runner and walls lined with original artwork in gaudy gold frames.

The end of the hallway opens to a library that is damn near the size of my one-bedroom apartment. Unlike my sparse apartment this stale space, with its oversized mahogany furniture, built-in bookshelves, and floor-to-ceiling drapes makes me feel like I might suffocate.

"Ms. Turner-Cosby will be available momentarily. If you'd like you can freshen up in the guest bathroom," he offers, pointing to a door on the opposite side of the room.

"I think I'm fresh enough. Thank you."

"Would you like a beverage?" he asks, offering to pour me a drink from a rolling bar cart.

"Water is fine."

Dante uncaps a bottle of Veen water, fills a glass and says, "Please make yourself comfortable, she won't be long."

I hadn't expected to have dinner but the aroma wafting into the room causes my stomach to growl, reminding me that I haven't eaten anything other than a few snacks at the bar.

Ms. Turner-Cosby enters the room in conversation on her cell phone, trailed by Dante who places a martini glass in her hand.

"Mr. Goodman, thank you for coming," she says, passing her phone off to Dante who then slithers his way out of the room.

"You're the client," I say, disguising my double take of her appearance with a sip from my glass of water.

There is a striking difference in her attire tonight from what she'd worn to my office earlier in the afternoon. Tonight she is dressed in a white jumpsuit with a deep front and back V-neck. A sash belt sits at her hips, and on her feet, a pair of Stubbs & Wooten hand-stitched velvet and gold monogrammed shoes. Ms. Turner-Cosby may be a shrewd businesswoman, proven to be capable of murder as well as blackmail, but she does it while dripping with class.

"I see Dante has made you comfortable," she says, suggestively curling her hair back behind one ear.

I hope she isn't sending a message other than being relaxed for a business dinner but the not-so-subtle signs are evident. Perhaps Hampton had been correct in his assumption of this woman.

"Yes, you have a beautiful home."

"Thank you. I prefer staying in town, as opposed to my family estate in Spring City. I've had enough country living for a while. As a matter of fact, you're the first man I've entertained since coming home."

"You mentioned having an additional business opportunity to discuss?"

"I thought we could eat first."

"I'm not hungry," I lie.

Disregarding my comments, her voice, in a tone softer than what I've become accustomed to, asks, "Don't you think Dante did a great job tending to my plants while I was away?"

"I'm sure Dante takes care of a lotta things," I respond, paying no attention to the two monstrous rubber trees that are blocking the glass doors to an outside patio.

I must've been correct in my assumption because her face flushes. Before she can gather a response, Dante enters the room with a silver tray, offering a warm towel for our hands. It feels like overkill but unfortunately, it's my new reality.

"Ma'am, dinner is ready."

"Mr. Goodman, shall we?"

I trail behind her into the formal dining room and she glances over her shoulder, offering a useless smile. It's clear that she doesn't have much of an ass but her body is in perfect shape. What catches me off guard is the scent of her perfume; it's the same fragrance her daughter wears.

In the formal dining room we take our seats at an overdone table set for two, with white china trimmed in gold, matching gold flatware and a different glass for whatever beverage I might choose.

"Ms. Turner-Cosby, I appreciate your hospitality but I'm not sure why you asked me here," I say noticing the tuna tartare hiding between slices of avocado. None of it appeals to me, as the only raw fish I eat is pussy.

"If you don't mind, I'd prefer not to discuss business until we finish our entrees. You could say it's one of my rules."

She keeps talking, mostly about Tiffany and how she'd like to merge their business and personal relationships, almost as if she were a commodity. I'm getting frustrated, especially since it's clear that Ms. Turner-Cosby has me here for reasons yet to be discussed.

That's when I notice her lack of eye contact. I decide to use it to my advantage.

"Rules? Ms. Turner-Cosby, let's not forget you're blackmailing me with some bullshit video you've compiled that can destroy everything I've built."

"You would've done the same if you were as passionate about something other than your fixation for watching women. Can you even explain how a man becomes obsessed with that?"

"Maybe we should eat," I respond, thinking that even if I wanted to explain, it wouldn't make a difference, plus it's none of her fuckin' business.

"I do admire your ability to guide my daughter in her business decisions."

"I wouldn't underestimate her. She's a smart woman. It's a profitable deal with low risks and a high return."

"I wish Tiffany could see other things that clearly."

"You want her to come public about your being her mother?"

"That's her decision. But if you could find a way to influence her, I'd make it financially rewarding."

"Don't you think some things should happen organically?"

"Perhaps she still needs time. Anyway, as for our business, an opportunity has become available that I'd like to extend to you."

With Dante standing guard, the servers enter the dining room, removing our appetizers and placing our entrée's before us at exactly the same moment.

"I'm listening," I say, unable to ignore the mouth-watering bone-in rib eye in front of me. As hungry as I am, even the mashed potatoes and multi-colored asparagus look irresistible. I don't even try to hide the fact that I'm starving and immediately cut into the steak. The juices run from its center.

"What if I can offer you the golden ticket?"

"Bilderberg?"

She nods and gives a soft smile.

The annual Bilderberg conference is intended to foster dialogue between Europe and North America but I know it does more than that. Its members are political leaders and experts from industry, finance and academia. The closest I've come to breaking into those ranks, was as a back-up speaker at the Bloomberg Global Business Forum two years ago.

I put my fork down. She has my attention.

"I thought it was made up by conspiracy theorist, sort of like the Illuminati," I lie, knowing that both organizations exist.

"As you're aware, my friends have unlimited amounts of cash and are always searching for a variety of ways to invest. If you travel with me, after convincing my daughter to accompany us, I can introduce you to people who can propel your firm into a global organization."

Traveling with these women to Bilderberg is an opportunity I wouldn't be able to garner on my own. If I decline, Hampton would kill me himself.

"And the video?"

"I'm sure we can find a way to resolve that after dinner."

I know exactly what that means and the thought of it fills me with dread. I've been with white women before but never any woman even close to the age of 60. Will her skin be wrinkled, her old pussy dry? If so, will Dante be called in to deliver some imported vaginal cream on a silver tray? What's worse is imagining in what ways she might be like her daughter—insatiable perhaps? To date, there have been no other circumstances where I had considered having sex with a mother and daughter. But if it's to my advantage, it's worth considering.

"Dante, can you please ask the chef to come out before she leaves? Actually Mr. Goodman, I believe you're familiar with my chef."

I'm so deep in my head wrangling with the idea of having to fuck this woman that when Zinzi enters the room I can barely speak.

"Evening," I stammer.

When she sees me, I can see the surprise and perhaps disappointment in her eyes that I am Ms. Cosby's dinner guest. Does she think I'm sleeping with this old woman? If so, why does she care? Our conversations to date have been focused on the culinary school but somehow I feel compelled to explain why she's serving me and why I'm here.

"Mr. Goodman, nice to see you again."

Turning her body and attention away from me she asks, "Ms. Turner-Cosby, have you enjoyed your meal?"

"Always Chef Z... always perfection. I appreciate you being available on such short notice. Dante will take care of you."

"Thank you. Enjoy your evening."

As Zinzi leaves the room, Ms. Cosby comments, "Chef Z's talent are in high-demand but you already know that."

This bitch is too deep into the crevices of my life, watching and knowing every move I make. I now know that it will never stop, nor will the video ever go away. At this point, Liek's proposition to bury her is becoming more of an option. She breaks my train of thought with, "Shall we adjourn to the library?"

I push back from the table and follow her back into the library where tall candles of varying heights flicker inside the stone fireplace. On the bar cart are two whiskey glasses engraved with "RTC," a silver ice bucket and a bottle of Dalmore 62. Fully aware that Dalmore is a rare single malt scotch but not really wanting to imbibe in her expensive liquor, I reason that it might help me complete the task at hand.

"I thought we might be more comfortable in here. Are you much of a bibliophile?" she asks, while crossing in front of me to entice me with her fragrance.

Perusing the shelves, I see several collections of rare books and original manuscripts. "It appears well-curated."

"Some of the books have been in my family for centuries."

"Is your family the reason why you gave Tiffany up for adoption?"

Her eyes cut across me so hard that if she had a gun I know I'd be her next victim.

"We're not here to discuss my family."

"Then why did you ask me here tonight?"

Tapping her glass against mine she says, "The answer to that should be obvious."

"Up until now you've been straightforward. Why not ask for what you want?"

Once again we've taken our positions, she beside the fireplace and me posted between the two club chairs.

"I'm in need of servicing, Mr. Goodman, and I believe you may be able to deliver."

"It's ironic that you warned me not to get personally involved with your daughter and yet here we are."

"Did you ever think that maybe I was saving you for myself? I mean I have watched that video several times."

I hadn't considered that.

"And that's how you ask to get fucked?" I ask, watching as her eyes go soft and vulnerable like her daughter.

"You don't think a woman my age can get you aroused?"

"Ms. Turner-Cosby, the only thing that gets my dick hard is money."

"I certainly have enough of that."

She goes to the bar cart to retrieve the bottle of Dalmore, refilling our glasses with the best scotch I've ever tasted.

"What you want comes at a price."

"Shall I have Dante bring you an envelope as well?" she asks, fingering the lapel of my sport coat.

"You already know the cost."

To get this over with, I pull the sash through the loops on her hips and reach behind her to unzip her jumpsuit, which falls from her shoulders.

"Would you like to go upstairs?"

"For what? I don't need a bed. Take that shit off."

While I sip on my drink, she sets her glass on the end table then, hesitating slightly, she steps out of her panties and unhooks her bra. Her body, although pale and sprinkled with freckles, hasn't fallen to gravity and I reason that the only thing fake, are her high-quality breast implants. Even naked she emanates power, but right now I'm holding all the cards.

"You see, it's not that bad," she says, pivoting to show me her ass. "And you Mr. Goodman? Exactly what am I getting?"

Since my dick is indeed hard, I undress while she watches.

"Impressive and..."

Before she can finish her sentence, I lift her up and carry her to the chaise lounge where she lay expecting more than she's going to get. Standing at the head of the chaise, my dick pointing in her face, I rub it across her lips until she opens her mouth.

"You sure this is what you want? I won't be gentle."

She answers by cupping my balls and taking them one at a time in her mouth, licking and kissing them until they are drenched with saliva. Then making a ring with her forefinger and thumb, she wraps them tightly around the rim of my dick and begins sucking on the head until droplets of cum trickle out. Her technique isn't that good but the effort she's making makes me admit that out of the many women I've observed sucking my dick, having Raquel Turner-Cosby's billion-dollar white lips wrapped around its head has to be the most gratifying.

Easing my dick out of her wet mouth she tells me, "I want this in me."

"Oh, you gone get it."

Rolling her over onto her stomach, I crook two fingers and roughly jam them inside her, causing her little clit to run for cover under its hood.

Back and forth, slow and fast, her body meets my fingers until I eventually have four of them inside her. When I lean over and allow her to kiss me, her milky orgasm slides down my hand. She is ready.

Positioning her on her knees, I use my tongue to lick up and down her freckled back. With her ass spread wide, I surprise her by plunging my dick inside, then pulling it out. I feel her trying to hold her breath and begin pummeling her pussy so hard she screams in what sounds like another language. For such an cultured woman, it just might be.

Unsure and not caring if she's screaming from pleasure or pain, I begin pounding her so hard the chaise moves and bangs against the floor.

"Is this what you wanted? You wanted me to fuck this ol' pussy?"

"Yes, yes it is...YES, O-H-H-H-H..."

Her escalating screams and the banging of the furniture brings a light tapping on the door.

"Ms. Cosby? Ms. Cosby, are you alright? Do you need me?" Dante implores from the other side of the door.

"I'm, I'm..."

"She's getting fucked," I yell back and with that, I run up in her again. This time her orgasm pours out, wetting up the chaise.

Wrapping a handful of her hair around my hands, I yank her head around and kiss her slow and deliberately as if we are making love. When I stop, she begs, "I wanna suck your dick, let me suck it please."

Taking a seat in the mess she's made on the chaise I tell her, "You know what to do, clean it up."

She positions herself on her knees in front of me and uses her tongue to lick every bit of her thick orgasm from between my thighs, under my balls, and the hairs covering them. Then she takes my dick in her mouth.

"Open your eyes," I tell her and once again she does as she's told. My dick swells in her mouth as she starts sucking it with so much fervor—and a little too much teeth—that I fear she's going to take the skin off. Ms. Cosby could definitely use some lessons from her daughter but nonetheless I am ready and give her full warning of her options.

Yanking her head back by her hair I tell her, "Listen bitch, if you don't swallow this nut I'm gonna slap the shit outta you, you understand?"

Just like her daughter, she swallows.

Chapter Nine

Zinzi

Under the premise of discussing the PR plan presented by Platinum Images for the opening of Zinzi's Culinary Institute, I'm able to convince Zinzi to have brunch with me. The one caveat: I have to do the cooking. I rarely spend time behind a stove, but for her I've offered myself up as her cook. For some reason I feel the burden of explaining myself to a woman I haven't even slept with.

I arrive at her place around 9:30 on Sunday morning, bringing with me fresh turkey sage sausage from Reading Terminal, home-fried potatoes with scallions and yellow peppers that my mother had prepped for me and all the fixings for a spinach and cremini mushroom omelet, my specialty.

"Morning, Bryce! Wow, look at all that! I can't believe you really agreed to cook."

"I'm a man of my word," I respond, noticing that she's come to the door wearing a vintage New York Giants T-shirt and gray sweat shorts displaying an ample ass for riding. Her hair is separated into two wild Afro puffs and they make me wonder if she has an Afro between her legs or if she's cleanly waxed. Either way I'm interested. A leather choker with a silver charm once again wraps around her neck and large silver hoops dangle off her ears.

Zinzi has only been in town for a few weeks, yet her apartment is completely unpacked and organized. The windows to her place are open with no blinds or curtains, and a multitude of houseplants combined with fresh herbs fill her wide windowsills. The kitchen counter holds a stack of cookbooks and a 15-inch flat screen television that is tuned to Enon Tabernacle's Sunday morning service.

With her seated on one side of the counter and me standing on the other near the stove, I toss the potatoes into a frying pan alongside the sausage. Full of enthusiasm, Zinzi updates me on the final phase of construction at her school, along with giving me detailed descriptions of its industrial kitchen appliances and tools, some of which I've never even heard of.

"So what's going on with you, Bryce?"

"Nothing with me. It's about you. Michael, our consultant at Platinum Images has scheduled interviews for you with local media, along with *Eater Philly* who's agreed to send someone to cover your grand opening. They'll also be providing someone to assist you with your social media campaign and keeping your website updated. Once you're ready, we'll confirm your interview with *Cook's*. How's that for starters?"

"Jeez, you work fast! Anything else I need to know before I get all blubbery?" she asks, her eyes bright with surprise.

"What would you think about Philly's top chef's teaching a class one night a week, along with hosting about 20 diners at $250 per plate that would go towards student scholarships?"

"When you say 'chefs' do you mean like Nick Elmi and Mark Vetri?"

I sprinkle the home fries with paprika then pull a sauté pan from her overhead pot rack and slowly start to brown the mushrooms in butter. "So far, they've confirmed Michael Solomonov and Greg Vernick."

"And they said yes?" she asks. I take note of the deep dimples in her cheeks.

"Of course they did, Michael and Shanté, who you've yet to meet, have made Zinzi's Culinary Institute a top priority," I tell her. In truth, my priority is getting Liek's money pushed through.

Smiling with her eyes and mouth she says, "You are amazing. Thank you, Bryce." She bounces off her stool to lean across the counter and intentionally kiss me on the cheek. "My staff will be overjoyed! Wait, you know we can't begin anything like that until next year. I have to get my footing first. But can I ask another favor, please?"

"I'm listening."

Luckily she hasn't mentioned my dinner with Ms. Cosby and I'm not about to bring it up. But I do need to know the basis of her relationship with Liek.

"Can we have a cheesesteak night? I mean we *are* in Philly, right? And I didn't think I would, but I love those things!"

"Whatever you want, they can make it happen."

With her hand pressed against her heavy breasts she exclaims, "Bryce, I don't know how to thank you."

I choose not to answer that loaded question and instead I focus on tilting the skillet to fold our omelet over before slipping it onto a plate.

"Oh, I have one more thing. I picked up a little housewarming gift," I say, before presenting her with an autographed copy of *Between Harlem and Heaven, Afro-Asian-American Cooking for Big Nights, Weeknights, and Every Day.*

"You're full of surprises!" she says as she thumbs through the pages. "This is beautiful. I've wanted this book, how'd you know? Thank you, Bryce."

I set her food down in front of her.

"This looks delicious! Very rarely do I get to have someone cook for *me*. Who taught you to cook?"

"My mother," I respond, watching her make love to every single bite of food she places in her mouth. "How is it that you're able to make watching you eat so enjoyable?"

"When I was growing up in Tortola my mother taught me how to use all of my senses when eating, absorbing it through the eyes and nose before it even touches my palate."

"You're from the British Virgin Islands?"

"Yes! People in the states have no idea what it's like growing up somewhere where it's always beautiful."

"You still have family there?"

"Lots of family and my parents have—well, they had—a small café, the Pleasant Pheasant. The hurricanes swept it away."

"Can it be rebuilt?"

"It's way too expensive and they're already battling with the insurance company."

I want to offer to help but don't want to overstep my bounds.

"Remember you said I should think about establishing a non-profit?" Zinzi begins. "What if I centered it around feeding homeless children and first responders, during disasters... that sort of thing?"

"You're a smart woman, Zinzi. That's the perfect platform. Why not call it the Pleasant Pheasant?"

"Really? You'd help with that too?"

"Without question."

We continue to eat in silence, I think partly because she is overcome with emotion on how her culinary school is taking on additional wings. Meanwhile, I'm trying to figure out how best to inquire about her relationship with Liek.

"Tell me your favorite food so I'll know what to cook next time." I say, not even sure why because the majority of my meals are eaten in restaurants.

"I eat everything, can't you tell?" she says, pinching her thick thighs. "You know what they say, thicker than a snicker..."

To avoid being inappropriate, I concentrate on watching her mix her fresh squeezed orange juice with some of the Veuve Cliquot I'd brought along.

"Why do you women do that?"

"What?"

"Find a way to criticize what others see as the best part of you. It's like you feel you don't deserve to be beautiful. Like, if one part of you is good, you have to point out something negative."

"Well, aren't you the observer! Speaking of which, why do you look at me like that anyway?"

"Like what?"

"Like you're studying me."

"Why do you always wear chokers?" I ask, assuming she might have an asphyxiation fetish.

"I don't know, I guess I like the pressure on my neck. It lets me know I'm alive."

She's definitely baiting me but I'm not falling for it, instead I begin scraping and stacking the dirty dishes in the dishwasher.

"Have you met them? They live upstairs in the penthouse."

I turn my eyes towards the television to see that she's referring to the Governor and Tiffany who are members of Enon Tabernacle. As guests in the pulpit, they are sitting beside Reverend Waller, advocating providing literary programs in churches across Pennsylvania.

"Actually, I've met them both," I reply, trying not to recall my intimate moments with the First Lady.

"Now, *she* looks like your type. She's quite pretty, almost looks like she's from the islands," observes Zinzi as the camera stays on Tiffany standing dutifully smiling next to her husband, as if what he has to say is all that matters.

"I don't have a type. As far as pretty, I'm a man that believes sexy is a far better trait then pretty, it lasts longer."

"If that's so, then what's your relationship with that Turner-Cosby woman? I overheard the two of you talking about her, are they related somehow?" she inquires, her eyes still glued to the television.

"They're clients," I answer, wondering exactly how much she'd overheard.

"Here's what I know," she counts off on her fingers, "One, when it comes to money there is no type and two, having now spent some time with you I can see there's more to Bryce Goodman than you portray. And three, as for your little dinner the other night, that wasn't business, that ol' lady had specifics. 'Romantic' was the request I received from Dante."

"I would never get into a personal relationship with a client."

"C'mon Bryce, men like you treat women like an amusement park; you get on all the rides and the ones you like the most you ride until the park closes. Then you get up and go home. Tell me that isn't what you do!"

Rather than feed into what she thinks, she knows about me, I turn the tables on her and ask, "Is Liek your type?"

"Now you're going to deflect? I was waiting for that question." She takes a sip of her mimosa. "I met Liek when I was at C.I.A."

"C.I.A?"

"Culinary Institute of America. Liek's company employed my baby brother," her downcast eyes immediately fill with sadness, "When Tally was murdered in a drive-by, Liek made himself my unofficial guardian. It was his idea I open a school. I was content just being a private chef."

"That's it? You and him?"

"If you're asking if I'm sleeping with him," a coy smile appears across her lips, "No."

There was something else. Is she repaying him by working in some other capacity?

"I haven't slept with him or anyone else. I'm virgin territory."

Relieved, I calculate how we might make time for each other barring our busy and unpredictable schedules. I'm so caught up in my thoughts that I don't fully understand what she means by virgin territory.

"Repeat that."

"I've never slept with or had sex with anyone. I'm a virgin," she confirms, stifling a girlish laugh behind her hand.

"I'm sorry, but how old are you?"

"33. Does that excite you? It does most men."

There is a simple rule among men about having sex with a virgin, especially one her age: Don't do it.

"No, that scares the shit outta me. I mean how did that happen?"

"I was in school focused on my goals, like I am now. A boyfriend would've been distracting for me. I've seen it happen over and over again, plus my parents are strict when it comes to education. And Liek, well, you know how he is. He's not going to let anybody get close to me without his approval."

"Does he know you're a virgin?"

"Of course not, we don't talk about that sort of stuff. He's constantly teasing me though about having a secret life. He probably thinks I like girls, which I don't. I just need a different kind of man."

Curious, I ask, "What kind of man appeals to you?"

"You know, the kind that brings home flowers with a loaf of French bread under his arm. I wanna be the woman a man looks forward to seeing at the end of the day. I know you're not that kind of man."

"What the fuck does that mean?"

"That hurt?"

"Yes, it does! What kind of man do you think I am?"

"You, Bryce Goodman, are 'The Alpha Male.'"

Chapter Ten

Optimal Play

My week has been loaded with meetings, conference calls, a trip to New York to meet with Liek, then to Atlanta with Hampton, where we signed the NBA's new power forward, Anthony Thomas.

Friday at 7:00 a.m. has me at the Pyramid Club, where I spend two hours over breakfast with a new client and her lawyer. Alaina Durdin, a local author, recently made news after optioning the movie rights to her books to Overbrook Entertainment. The seven-figure deal left her turning to the Goodman Firm to determine how best to invest and grow her newfound money.

Leaving there I take an Uber to 30th Street Station to meet my mother for a day trip to Washington, DC to tour the National Museum of African American Culture. We spend three hours touring each floor then meet up with family members for an early dinner at Fiola's before returning to Philly.

Saturday morning Hampton and I fly in Ms. Cosby's private jet to Ligonier, PA to play in the Triple D Invitational golf tournament hosted in part by RTC Holdings at Laurel Valley Golf Club. Another instance where being in business and, unbeknownst to others, in bed with her is paying off.

Hampton is a serious golfer with a handicap of three, which means I'm not even included in his foursome. My swing isn't bad but I mainly play to build business relationships, making it a good balance of our time out of the office.

Later that evening back in Philly, I change into a tux to attend the Union League's Formal Cigar Event, where I find myself in an awkward conversation with Governor Skinner. The man is an upstanding politician and a well-portrayed family man, with eyes on 1600 Pennsylvania Avenue, making it even harder for me to understand why he's willing to share his wife with others. Presumably, he doesn't know I'm one of them.

It's after midnight when members start on another level of drinking. I've ignored two phone calls from Ms. Turner-Cosby inviting me to stop by her house after the event. It isn't the worst invitation but I'm too damn tired; I just want to go home and sleep before my workweek begins in 24 hours. She isn't big on text messages but I send one anyway suggesting an early dinner at her house on Sunday.

Stepping outside onto Broad Street, I make the short walk to my apartment. My phone vibrates.

Tiffany: your dick, my mouth, ten minutes

Me: unlock your door

I'm not sure where Governor Skinner is spending the night, but I make my way to punish his wife for sending those types of messages. I don't fully trust her—or her mother—having entrapped me in a web of wealth and sex and for that they have to pay.

Having now been at the Divine Lorraine several times, the concierge no longer asks where I'm going. He just throws a thumbs up when I arrive.

Tiffany hasn't lied, her door is unlocked and she is naked. Ten minutes after my arrival, my dick is in her mouth.

"Is that all you got for the night?" she asks after I empty my load in her mouth.

"Depends on how good you are," I respond, stepping out of my pants and following behind her into the living room.

She takes a seat on the couch so she is sitting across from me, naked. Her legs are propped on the coffee table and spread wide, giving me a view of her beautifully waxed pussy. Casually she lights a joint, takes a puff and passes it to me. She picks up the remote, hits play and Stephanie Mills and Teddy croon, "Feel the Fire." I can't recall the last time I've heard a Teddy Pendergrass song. She has a full playlist.

"I hope you feel like having fun tonight."

"Stop talking and let me see that ass you sitting on."

"This what you want?" she asks, amazing me by shoving two fingers inside her pussy all the way up to her knuckles.

"That's one pretty pussy. Show me some more."

She takes the bait, spits into the palms of both hands and uses them to brush against her nipples until they harden.

"I wanna know what it feels like be your whore," she says.

I'm not sure this is a game she plays with the governor but its one I'm used to. It also makes me realize that for as much as this bitch and her mother try to control me, it's actually them who need to be controlled.

"Are you capable?" she asks with a smile that's so dangerously sexy I tell myself that whatever submissive games this bitch wants to play, I'm her man.

"Bitch, fill my glass and take your hair out that fuckin' bun."

She removes the hairpins and then the band that holds it in. When her hair falls from place, my dick starts to twitch. So this is what she looks like when she isn't in the public eye.

I puff on the joint and she uncorks another bottle of Dom. She refills our glasses, I down mine and hold my glass out for another. Determined to fulfill her request for me to treat her like my whore, when I feel the pressure building, I stand over her and pull on my dick until drops of pee trickle onto her stomach. She finds it amusing and when she begins to laugh I point my dick towards her mouth. When the warm piss sprays all over her face, her eyes open as wide as her mouth.

"Now be a good whore and clean it up."

When she finishes licking away the pee from her lips and my dick, I take what remains of the champagne and pour it over her breasts. Back and forth from one to the other I suck them so hard she digs her nails into my neck screaming my name, until without warning I shove my hard dick inside her, allowing her to release another orgasm.

"How'd you get so fucken nasty?"

"You bring it outta me. Now sit down. I wanna show you something."

Taking a seat on the sofa I listen to Teddy's smooth voice telling us, "...*Let's get lost in each other...*" On the coffee table, she raises herself up on her knees and rotates her ass in small circles, teasing me.

"Keep it right there," I tell her. With both hands, I grab a head full of her hair and say, "Push that ass out to me." When she does, I go down on my knees behind her and lick from the pink eye of her spicy asshole all the way to the soft flesh of her sweet pussy.

My dick is so swollen that when I stand up to enter her, I can barely get it inside. But she keeps pushing her ass back to me and I keep grinding down until her pussy opens up and sucks my dick in like a vacuum. It's so hot in there and I'm fucking her so savagely I must force myself to slow down before I show too soon.

Grabbing hold of her fat breasts, I spit between the fat cheeks of her ass, making it easy to use the head of my dick to test her tender asshole. As I watch the head of my dick angling its way inside, I can feel her ass begin to spread. That's when I push my way inside with all my force.

"OH MY GOD YOU.... you..." she turns her head to the side and begs to know, "Bryce, why are you fucking me like this?"

"Shut up and take this dick, you dirty whore. You know you like it when it hurts don't you."

"Yes, yes, it hurts but...it's my ass...what the..."

And just like that I pull it out and jam it back in her waiting pussy, surprising myself by releasing a nut so hard that I collapse on top of her.

"You had enough now?" I ask thirty minutes later as we lay spent on the floor.

"I wanna make love to you."

"Tiffany, I ain't got nothing left."

"Yes, you do."

Hopefully, she doesn't see the surprise on my face, because I have no idea what she's talking about. This woman is relentless.

She asks me to light another joint, while she goes in the kitchen to pop another bottle of champagne. How many bottles of this shit does she have? We've already gone through three.

Holding up my limp dick, I say, "Listen, if you can get this thing hard again, it's all yours."

"Well then, I guess you better leave it to me."

In between drinking and smoking, Tiffany starts out slow, almost without me noticing her using her hands, to massage my shoulders then my chest and down my thighs. When her legs straddle me and the stickiness of her body rubs against my stomach, I find myself praying to get hard again.

In between me telling her what I'm going to do to her, she kisses me with so much intensity and tenderness that somewhere deep in my balls I swear I can feel my sperm gathering to make another run for it.

Her mouth rounds my biceps, down the center of my back, to the rounds of my ass and if I'd ever had any opposition to it, I don't even flinch when her tongue laps my asshole. Her tactics are so strategic in making my dick hard, that I can no longer lay on my stomach.

She gets what she wants and after having viciously fucked all over her apartment, we find ourselves practically glued together with body fluids between the doorway of her bedroom and living room. Taking my cue from Teddy who is now telling us, "...*Two a.m. when the party's over...I wanna be with you...*" I'm tempted to see how much more she can take.

"Go get my belt," I tell her.

With that pretty ass touted up in the air she crawls over to the couch, pulls my belt from in between the cushions, and slings it around her neck. Then with two fingers I beckon her to crawl back to me.

I hook the belt, tight around her neck and watch her eyes beg for whatever I'm going to do next. Throwing her legs over my shoulders, my body leans forward onto her thighs, pushing them downward, making it easy for me to take turns penetrating whatever hole I chose and with each thrust inside her I tighten the belt and she rewards me with her juices. By now her dark skin is moist with sweat, and her hair matted to her face. Her eyes bore so deep into mine, I have to blink because in that moment it's hard for me not to tell this bitch I love her.

Instead, through gritted teeth I say, "I own this pussy, you fuckin' hear me, you stinking whore?"

She's panting too hard to respond.

"You hear me? I'm gonna fuck the shit outta you every time I see you."

This time her eyes flash open but instead of them being filled with lust, they roll back in her head.

"What the fuck?"

Releasing my grip on her neck, I quickly unhook the belt. "Hey, you ok?"

When she doesn't answer I get closer to her face and ask again, "Hey, hey," and this time when she doesn't answer I realize she's barely breathing.

"HEY! ANSWER ME!"

Still no movement.

My dick goes soft and slips from inside her. Her legs drop onto the floor. She's motionless. What the fuck happened? Had she taken something before I arrived? Had she laced the weed we'd been smoking and the champagne we'd been drinking, is that why my dick continued to rise three, four times?

Slapping her back and forth with the open palm of my hand, I beg.

"FUCK! FUCK! Look at me, open your eyes!"

Floundering desperately, I try giving her mouth-to-mouth but I've never taken a CPR class. I think about chest compressions, but I'll only be banging on her chest, and it doesn't help that I'm now being taunted by Teddy, "...bad luck, that's what you got, that's what you got..."

I can't let her die; she's the governor's wife, the First Lady of Pennsylvania. From the phone on her nightstand, I press 911, giving them the address and apartment number, then foregoing the consequences; I call her mother.

Fortunately, the fire departments medic unit arrives in less than five minutes of my call, not even giving me enough time to get dressed.

As luck would have it, the lead paramedic turns out to not only be a client, but Shanté's nerdy boyfriend, Tyrone. This night just keeps getting worse. He gives me a knowing nod.

Placing his stethoscope between Tiffany's sweaty breasts, Tyrone listens while the other tech named Briana checks her pulse.

"I got a pulse but it's faint."

"Heartbeat is rapid. Blood pressure is 170 over 110. Let's prop her head."

Briana pulls a pillow from the bed and places it under Tiffany's head.

Tyrone flashes a penlight across Tiffany's eyes.

"Let's hook her up."

Following Tyrone's orders Briana tears open a blue oxygen mask and passes it to him.

"Do you have something we can cover her with?"

What does that mean? Is she dead? Had I fucked her to death?

I scan the room and grab a sheet hanging off the bed. I hand it to her.

"What's her name?"

They already know she's the governor's wife, everyone knows. They've been in the public eye for over 10 years.

"Tiffany Johnson-Skinner," I mumble, my mind in a state of befuddlement.

I kneel at Tiffany's feet.

"When did she lose consciousness?" Briana asks me.

"Can you tell us what happened? How long has she been like this?"

As she asks questions, Briana surveys the bedroom, casting a disapproving look at me. There's shit everywhere, we're both naked and the apartment smells of piss, sex, weed, liquor and my damn belt is still behind her neck.

Tyrone inserts an IV and Briana holds the bag up while she continues firing questions at me; asking her age, date of birth, if she has any allergies or preexisting medical conditions.

What can I tell them? I don't know anything about this woman beyond her investments and the personal satisfaction she gives me.

"Has she been drinking?"

I nod yes.

"Any drugs?"

Panic is setting in, making me feel like I might pass out.

"NO, no drugs."

"Sir, I need you to focus. What's your name?"

"My...my...name," I stutter, so caught up in what or what not to tell them that I don't even realize that Ms. Turner-Cosby has entered the room. On her heels is the ever-present Dante, followed by a man who identifies himself as Dr. Strohmile.

The medics make room for the doctor, who kneels down next to Briana. He checks Tiffany's vital signs. Ms. Turner-Cosby snaps her attention toward me.

"YOU DID THIS! YOU FUCKED MY DAUGHTER! I WARNED YOU! I WILL MAKE SURE YOU LOSE EVERYTING! YOU HEAR ME? THE WORLD WILL SEE THAT VIDEO, YOU PIECE OF SHIT. EVERYONE WILL KNOW WHO YOU ARE!"

"Ms. Turner...Cosby, I can explain, let me explain," I beg, even though I know there is no explanation for what has happened. She doesn't give me a chance anyway. Her flailing arms slap at my face. I block her with my hands as her open palms turn into fists, her knuckles smacking repeatedly against my left jaw. During all of this her feet kick to make contact with my exposed dick.

"Ms. Turner-Cosby!" I yell, trying to shield her blows and to remind myself she is a woman lest I cold-cock the shit out of her. Luckily, for both our sakes, Dante and Tyrone drag her away just in time. Then Dr. Strohmile calls out, "Ms. Turner-Cosby, I think she's coming to."

Crying, Ms. Turner-Cosby falls to her knees beside Tiffany, her hands smoothing back the hair that is stuck to her daughter's face.

"Tiffany, it's me... it's me. Please wake up; it's your mother. Please don't leave me. I love you. I've always loved you."

I don't know if it's the sound of her mother's voice but Tiffany's blinking eyes start to show signs that she's regaining consciousness.

Ms. Turner-Cosby's reddened face with its bulging blue veins, turn to me. "Leave now. Do you hear me? GET THE HELL OUT! GET OUT AND SOMEBODY TURN THAT FUCKING MUSIC OFF!"

I hurry into the living room to hear Teddy's warning, *"...don't let this cold, cold, world get you down..."*

I gather up my pants and jacket from the hallway, and my tuxedo shirt and underwear from under the coffee table. My shoes, I need my shoes! I can't find them. I search the kitchen, bathroom, dining room and then back in the living room I reach under the couch, where I pull out one shoe and two black socks. Where is my other fucking shoe? I decide not to search for it; I have to get out of here before this woman kills me. Pulling my cell phone from between the couch cushions, I gaze into the bedroom.

I see Tyrone and Briana packing everything up, Dr. Strohmile kneeling at Tiffany's feet. And the infamous Raquel Turner-Cosby is cradling her daughter, the naked and barely conscious governor's wife. I slide my phone out of my pocket and press record. This video just may prove to be my way out of this spider's web.

Chapter Eleven

9-1-1

The last thing I want to do is personally hurt or publically embarrass Tiffany but unfortunately she's about to become collateral damage.

My only advantage is that Ms. Turner-Cosby's first priority will be to protect her daughter by keeping the incident out of the media. She also can't risk exposing me before they make the public announcement of her NFL team purchase, especially since it's linked to The Goodman Firm.

If she does release the video, I wonder if they will distribute footage of my activities anonymously or if she'll want to take credit for destroying me. Surely she has the means to turn this to her advantage. Either way I dread waking up one morning to a barrage of voicemails that Bryce Goodman has become another monster in the #MeToo movement.

With my head grappling with a million scenarios, I can't sleep and this is definitely no time to be drinking. I hate to admit it but I can't figure this out on my own. I need help coming up with a strategy.

Monday morning when I step out the elevator at 7:00 a.m., I find Shanté standing behind the reception desk anticipating my arrival.

"Boss, we need to talk."

She takes a seat in one of the visitor's chairs and pats the other for me to do the same.

"What the hell happened on Saturday? That woman gave Tyrone and Briana five thousand dollars each and made them sign an N.D.A. not to talk. I told them not to spend a fuckin' penny of that money until I talk to you."

"I'll sweeten the pot with another five K and something for you too."

"First of all, you ain't gotta give me or them shit. But seriously, what happened? Tyrone said the governor's wife is Ms. Turner-Cosby's daughter? That doesn't even make sense, I mean one bitch is black and the other bitch is white, and she's talking 'bout destroying you. Is that shit for real? I know you ain't letting that shit happen."

"Relax Shanté, I'll figure it out but right now you're the only one who knows and I need your help."

"Whatever you need, Boss, you know I got you."

"Schedule a meeting for this evening at six o'clock, with Michael, Reds, Hampton, my mother, yourself and Thomas. Tell him to bring the Rainmaker. One more thing, get Liek on the phone for me."

"They're gonna wanna know why we're meeting."

"9-1-1."

"Boss--"

"Yea, what's up?" I ask as I make my way towards my office.

Removing her glasses and giving me the slowest neck roll I've ever seen on a Black woman, she adds, "I ain't know you was killing it *like that*! You a Boss, for real!"

For the first time in three days, Shanté makes me laugh.

For the remainder of the day, I immerse myself in work. At the top of my To Do list is reviewing CV's for new brokers. Our business is growing at a pace neither of us expected and we no longer have the bandwidth to personally service each client. On my schedule, in addition to several client meetings, are documents to sort through on the requirements for Tiffany to be approved for the Giving Pledge, which I already know need Ms. Turner-Cosby's endorsement. I also have a private lunch meeting at Zahav with Chef Solomonov, to discuss arrangements for a dinner party I'm planning for Zinzi's family when they arrive from Tortola. All of this has to be done while I keep a watchful eye on an unsteady stock market. I can't afford the market *and* my life, to crash simultaneously. In the midst of it all comes the call from Liek.

"Bry man, what's up? Everything good?"

"No," I say trying to figure out how to phrase my request. "How much notice do you need to send your business partners to Philly to assist with that project we spoke of?"

He hesitates. I wait, hoping he catches on.

"They can be there tonight, just give me the name and when you ready for them to make a move. All you gotta do is text 9-1-1."

"Raquel Turner-Cosby."

"Shit, man. That's high cotton. You can't hesitate on that shit cause she *will* fuck your shit up, which means fucking up my shit, and that's not good for nobody. So you need to make your move before she do."

"I understand. Wait for my text."

At 5:45 I walk into the conference room. Each anxious face around the table asks the same question, "Why are we here?"

I realize at that moment there's no way I can tell them what's on the tape. Liek is right. I have to pull the trigger before she does.

The most worried face among them that I can't ignore is my mother's. With her hands laced in front of her, Mary Goodman looks as if she's just finished praying. Knowing my mother, I'm pretty sure she has.

Shanté of course is scrolling through social media on her cell phone, confident that she has more details than anyone.

Thomas, my lawyer who reviews every contract at the Goodman Firm and Maddox Investments, stares straight at me as if he can pry the words out of my mouth before I can speak them.

Next to him is the firm's forensic accountant, Lisette, who we affectionately refer to as Reds because of her hair color.

Michael, iPad in hand, stands off in the corner closest to the door, ready at a moment's notice to run out and assemble his staff of fixers.

The "Rainmaker," attorney Mr. Theodore Mohammed, is obviously in no hurry. Each hour spent at our office earns him $650. I know that once I speak with him privately, he'll suggest I put him on retainer.

Of all of the people gathered at the table, Hampton appears the most anxious. Rather than wait for me to launch into my statement, he blurts out, "Man, what the hell is going on?"

"Let me first say I appreciate everyone coming together on short notice. The thing is, recently I made some bad decisions and put myself, and subsequently the firm, in a compromising position. As ridiculous as it may seem, there's a video. I can honestly tell you that I haven't done anything illegal, but my actions, if publicized, could put the firm's business dealings under scrutiny, which could lead to a federal investigation and perhaps personal lawsuits and..." I pause, trying not to let any emotion show, then add, "the freezing of our assets."

"You wanna tell me what she's got on you?" Hampton asks.

"I'm reluctant to discuss too much because I don't want anyone being liable. Once I meet with Mr. Mohammed privately, he'll give us instructions on how to proceed if this situation does indeed come to light."

"Who is *she*?" my mother asks, the words barely coming behind her tight lips.

"Raquel Turner-Cosby."

"Shit," I hear Thomas mumble.

"The other threat," I look around the room knowing they all are bound by non-disclosures and all of whom I trust, I continue, "is the governor's wife." The fact that she is Ms. Turner-Cosby's biological daughter need not be revealed at this point.

"Shit," Thomas mumbles again.

"What about the Panthers deal? Those numbers are locked in," whispers Reds, her eyes twinkling with ways to move money without giving off red flags.

"Wait, we own an NFL team?" inquires Shanté.

I nod yes.

"Her press conference is today, she's bringing Mike Tomlin on as her GM," offers Hampton who has been the lead on the deal from our end.

"The NFL won't take kindly to any kind of problems and it sounds like this would be a big one. The way we structured the contract, she'd have to concede ownership to the governor's wife, which means us. But if she tries to take us down—"

"Stop it! No one is taking my son down."

"Mom."

"I don't care how rich she is. She's no better—and definitely no smarter—than you and the people around this table. So do what you have to, but fix it, son. Because I won't let a woman, especially, a white woman ruin the Goodman name. You hear me?"

Mr. Mohammed speaks, "I agree with you, Mrs. Goodman. Once your son and I speak we'll let everyone know what the next steps are." He looks around the conference table, his eyes land on Shanté, "Word will come from Ms. Miller."

Directing his attention to Mr. Mohammed, Michael states, "Whatever you give me, my team will craft a response for the key clients, and sound bites for the media. I assume Hampton should be the spokesman?"

"No," I say, "I'll do whatever speaking is necessary."

"Bry, you know I trust you but please tell me you have a play. We got a lot at stake here," begs Hampton.

"I think I have us covered but it's not something I want to use."

"Understood."

"I suggest you keep a low profile until we determine her next move," offers Michael.

"I can find out," says Mr. Mohammed, adding, "But he's right, stay out of the public view for a few days."

"That won't be easy, we have client meetings and I...."

"Man, fuck that, I can cover this shit, " says Hampton.

"So while the Boss is keeping a low profile what are we supposed to do?"

"Son, where will you go?"

"I don't know but I'll only be making two phones calls while I'm away."

Chapter Twelve

Virgin Territory

Desperately needing to get out of Philly, I decide I don't want to go alone. I need a distraction, something to take my mind off of everything that's happening. My thoughts turn to Zinzi. The construction on the school has been completed, the appliances are all in and she's fully staffed. Her current focus is on fine-tuning the curriculum. I decide to take my chances and call her that night.

"Hey Bryce, what's up? I hope you're calling to schedule dinner?"

"Actually, I'd like to schedule about three dinners, all of which will require your discerning expertise."

"Sounds intriguing."

"There's a client of mine, opening a restaurant in Collingswood, and he'd like to hire you to do the final tasting for his new chef," I lie, not even knowing where the lie came from.

"Great! I don't know where Collingswood is but I'm up for it."

"That's the thing, Collingswood is over the bridge in Jersey but the chef is still at another restaurant so we'll need to leave town tomorrow for about two, maybe three days."

"You can't be serious! You know I can't leave right now. This place is crazy, I'm sorry, Bryce, I'd really like to but not now, maybe in a few months."

"That's the reason why it'd be a good idea. It'll give your team a chance to sort things in your absence then you can see what they're really made of. Plus it'll be your last opportunity to slow down and get some perspective on things. We can even put our heads together to draft a mission statement for your foundation."

I'm sure I sound desperate but the lies keep coming, "The fee would be somewhere around twenty-five hundred to three-thousand, and the trip would be first class."

The quiet makes me know she's considering it.

"Ok, I'm in. But we can't leave until tomorrow afternoon."

Initially, I'm unsure of where to take her. Hampton suggests St. Barts or Tulum, Mexico. Then I realize I have the perfect place, River Maddox.

* * *

After a first class flight to Denver then another into Telluride, we pull up to the banks of River Maddox. Unbeknownst to the welcoming staff and certainly to Zinzi, River Maddox is held under my private company, Maddox Investments. I've never taken the time to visit, but it had been a low-risk investment that continues to turn a big profit. Despite my ownership, I've paid full price for this week and will be "glamping" among the 50 other guests.

As our personal staffer unloads our luggage and shows us to our tent, Zinzi's first question is, "We're going camping?"

"Not like you'd imagine," I say, taking note of the tents, large and small, that scatter the riverbank.

"Bryce, this place is beautiful but let's not lose focus. We're here on business."

If she's referring to us getting intimate, after my experience with Tiffany, the mere thought of the energy and emotion it would take to break in a 33-year-old virgin doesn't even excite me.

Pressing my finger against her lips I say, "I'm good."

Judging by Zinzi's reaction to our accommodations, it's well worth the money I've spent. Included in our Stargazer package is a secluded oversized tent, outfitted with a full bathroom, deck, king-size bed with an overhead viewing window and a wood-burning stove. If I thought she was impressed with our accommodations, she's even more impressed to learn that gourmet chefs will be preparing the majority of our meals.

Our first night together includes a welcome reception then bar-b-que and bourbon. After we retire to the tent, I lay awake contemplating what could be happening back home. Zinzi, who earlier made no resistance to our sharing a bed, curls up underneath me and falls asleep.

The next day I awake to Zinzi sitting at the edge of the bed and offering me a cup of coffee.

"Morning. What time is it?"

"It's going on eight o'clock. Hope you're hungry because the breakfast buffet is amazing and we have a full day."

Sitting up to take a sip of coffee, I ask, "Really, what are we doing?"

"After breakfast, we're going on a four wheeler ride through the mountains, and then we can either go fishing, canoeing, hiking, whatever you want. Oh, for lunch there's a big picnic at the lake and tonight there's wine tasting with dancing under the stars. You do dance, don't you? What about swimming? Do you know how to swim? Because tomorrow..."

Maybe it has something to do with her being a virgin but up until now the Zinzi I'd come to know was all about business. But today, in this place she's excited and I'm enjoying it. Maybe she needs this trip as much as I do, except for different reasons.

"Slow down, let's just work on today. How's this? I'll do whatever you want but there's one thing I must do, I have to make a call."

"To those witches? You know they have a spell on you? Women do it all the time back home. It's easy. All it takes is a little bit of sex and, for you, a whole lotta money."

"Zinzi, I can explain my relationship with them," I respond, not even sure what I'm going to say and furthermore what I might say if I need to explain my downfall.

Placing her hands over her ears she says, "I don't want to hear your explanation 'cause it's only gonna be lies."

"I really can explain."

"Listen, Bryce, I agreed to come here with you on business. Go on, call who you need to but hurry back to me."

While Zinzi's eats breakfast, I hop on a four-wheeler and head away from the camp until my phone vibrates with text messages and voicemail notifications. Among the voicemails are two from Ms. Cosby.

Show time. I make the call.

"Bryce here."

"Mr. Goodman. Wherever you've disappeared to, I suggest you stay there. It's over for you. If I were you, I'd prepare myself for the worse."

Eager to make her realize that we are both culpable in this situation, I reply, "I'm not sure exposing me is your best move."

"And I'm not someone you should be threatening."

"I suggest you check your phone for an incoming video. After that, if you have any questions, you can direct them to my attorney, Theodore Mohammed."

"Excuse me?"

"Check your phone. Talk to you soon."

If after receiving my footage she's still intent on destroying me, then Mr. Mohammed has a plan on how to proceed, and so does Liek. Meanwhile, I plan to enjoy my time at River Maddox.

I drive the ATV back to meet Zinzi where we spend the day trekking through the mountains, horseback riding and white water rafting down the San Miguel River. We both decline an offer to go into Telluride for shopping and dining, and opt for the picnic instead.

Later in the afternoon we return to our campsite to prepare for a 7:00 p.m. dinner. Guests have been urged to wear white, with shoes being optional. Zinzi is beautiful in a simple sleeveless, white linen dress that stops at her ankles and she smells incredible. "Honey blossom," she calls it. I haven't packed anything white, so my knee-length cargo shorts and short sleeve linen shirt will have to suffice. We both go without shoes.

For our dinner under the stars, there is no tent, only five, ten-foot long, linen-laid tables on a raised wooden platform. The music is a mix of R&B and Rock and Roll, which seems to please all the guests. Tonight will also be a lesson, taught by Zinzi, in learning how to properly savor food.

Each course for the evening is paired with a different wine, beginning with a crisp Santa Margherita Pinot Grigio, along with a massive amount of hors d'oeuvres. I keep going back for the lobster toasts with avocado.

Zinzi can't get enough of the seared lettuce cups. "If the chef prepared these," she takes another little bite, "they are perfect. It's not easy to get the right balance of ginger and lime juice, and know how to keep the steak warm."

When I suggest that the dressing on our locally sourced mixed greens is sugar, Zinzi explains to me the way in which to truly taste my food.

She dips the tip of a spoon in the dressing, "Taste it," she says and I do. "Now slowly glide your tongue along the roof of your mouth, like this," she says, demonstrating with her own tongue.

"Honey?"

"Even better. Truffle honey."

"Why can't I just lick my lips?"

"'Cause not all taste buds are located on the tongue. Some are found on the roof of the mouth and in the throat."

I wonder if this is her way of teasing me. I start feeling a buzz from my second glass of wine, a Sauvignon Blanc by Duckhorn, and promise myself to taste anything she offers.

When our entrees are set before us, a crab-stuffed lamp chop for me and for her a grilled trout, she gives me another lesson.

"Slow down, Bryce. I want to show you something. Flavor is counter-intuitive, less than 10 percent is taste and more than 90 percent is smell. I want you to close your eyes and take a slow deep breath."

After taking a sip of our third wine, a delicious Jordan Cabernet, I say, "Why don't you show me first?"

"Ok, here place something in my mouth."

All I can do is smile.

"You're so nasty. Here, take the fork and feed me something."

I do as she instructs, placing a little bit of trout on her fork and in her open mouth. She breathes in deep through her nostrils, takes the food on the tip of her tongue, and closes her mouth and her eyes. When she opens them, she details each fresh herb used to prepare her meal. Another balance, she calls it, of not wanting to overpower the freshness of the fish with a ridiculous amount of herbs.

"You can tell your friend his chef has my vote."

"The chef?" I ask, not recalling the lie I'd told her to get her here. It makes me realize we've yet to talk business at all.

"The chef you wanted me to check out for your client?"

"Right, of course, and I'll make sure you get your fee," I tell her knowing I'll be the one to cut the check.

"I'll write up my feedback on the flight back home. Is that okay?"

"Sure, perfect."

Zinzi schooling me catches on with the other guests and I watch her easily engaging them and telling them more about Zinzi's Culinary Institute. Her enthusiasm catches the attention of the evening's celebrity, Chef Janelle Boston. As I listen to her, I wonder if she even realizes how these people, as well as myself, are taken in by her infectious personality.

By dessert, we're both stuffed. After feeding each other a warm gingerbread and caramelized apple tart, I suggest we go for a walk.

Taking her by the hand, I ease Zinzi away from our new friends and towards the grass but I feel her pulling me back, asking, "Can we dance first?"

A funky old tune by the Rolling Stones, "Beast of Burden," plays. The lyrics are perfect but I'm unsure what moves to make to this beat. I think of a quote from former President Obama to "stay in the pocket" but then the music slows down.

I place my right hand on her lower back and the other on her shoulder. She wraps her arms around my waist, our bodies perfectly aligned.

"Does this work for you?" she asks, tugging me in tighter.

I plant a kiss on her forehead and say, "I like it. And I'm starting to like you very much, Chef Z."

I've never considered myself much of a romantic, but tonight the warm air, the music, the food and the scent of that damn honey blossom she's wearing have my feet completely out of step.

Her eyes are all smiles as she cocks her head to one side and teases, "I knew you couldn't dance."

In an attempt to prove her wrong, I take her hand in mine, step back, twirl her around then pull her in close enough for what she thinks will be a kiss. Instead I croon softly in her ear.

"...I started to believe I'd never find anyone...a one in a million chance of a lifetime...life showed *compassion...sent me a stroke of love called you...one in a million you...*"

At the sound of my voice, her eyes widen, amazed that I can hold a note.

"Bryce, I had no idea! You see what the beauty of nature can do?" She kisses my neck, snuggles in closer and whispers, "Thanks for bringing me here."

She's right. I can't recall ever having seen so many stars, not in Philly or on a Caribbean vacation. Tonight, they've all landed here, making this the most romantic night of my life. At this point, I let it all go, clients, women and fantasies, and reason with myself that maybe I can be the kind of man that brings home fresh flowers and French bread.

With her breasts pressed against my thin linen shirt, I bury my face in her hair and try to ignore the rising hardness of my dick, which for the first time embarrasses me. Zinzi reaches up and brushes her hands against the stubble of my outgrowing beard. In sync, our heads lean in together for our first kiss.

The song and our kiss ends, but it's hardly the end of our night. I could stay and dance with her some more, maybe even go for that walk, instead she leads me by the hand back to the Stargazer.

"You sure you want to do this, give yourself to me?" I ask as she stands under the skylight of our bedroom.

Using her hands to outline her voluptuous figure she says, "The question is, are you sure you want all this? I'm a lotta woman."

Holding her face in my hands I say, "I plan to make love to every inch of this thick sexy body, you hear me?"

She kisses me. "I didn't expect that."

Fingering my hands through her hair, I pull apart each of her kinky twists until her hair fluffs out like a crown over her head. Carefully I remove her choker, kiss her neck. After removing her earrings, I kiss her earlobes.

"You okay?"

"A little anxious but I think you're more nervous than I am."

It's not that I'm nervous, but I want to be sure I pay attention to all her verbal—as well as non-verbal—cues. I want to make this a night she'll be happy to remember.

Standing behind her, I unzip her dress, pulling it over her head. Before unhooking her bra, I push my hands up under its cups. I gently massage and push her breasts together to increase their sensitivity while kissing around her neck line and rubbing my dick against her back.

"You know I been waiting to get my hands on these," I say.

"They're all yours and so is the rest of me."

With Zinzi's fat breasts now turned to face me, my tongue licks around the outermost tip of her left nipple then the right. When she pushes them forward, my mouth devours the outermost roundness of each.

Teasing her, I remove my lips and I place them back onto her breasts. The cool air coupled with my saliva makes her nipples harden and swell, littering her body with goose bumps. At that moment, I fight to restrain myself. The beast in me wants to flip her over and bust her open. I quell those thoughts by sliding my tongue between her sweat-beaded breasts, all the way up her neck, until I reach her lips. She hungrily pulls me in for kiss.

"Bryce...I think...I think I'm ready," she says into my mouth.

"Slow down. Let me get my clothes off," I reply, bringing laughter from the both of us.

Once I'm naked, Zinzi reaches over and gives my dick a gentle tug. When she tries to take it in her mouth, I step away.

"We got plenty of time for that. It's about you tonight. But you gotta let me know if I'm hurting you, alright?"

She smiles, displaying those deep dimples. "I'm so glad I waited for you."

Turning away from me, she crawls back onto the bed. I can't help but be enticed by the arch of her spine, seeing it give way to enough hips and ass to loan somebody. Before I can stop myself, I grab her hips and yank her back down. Kneeling behind her, I run my tongue up and down the crack of her ass while I delicately stroke that secret space between her clit and her opening. With her body trembling and her juices soaking up my fingers, I realize that any woman less than her size can't match the satisfaction she's already given me.

Zinzi lies back on the bed and I move down to the hair covering the mound of what is soon to be mine. Rubbing my face and lips all in it, I soak up the warmth of her body. The sweat from her thighs brings back the sweet taste of the caramelized apples we've just eaten.

"What's happening, on my God, what's happening?" she cries out, her hands guiding my head to what she enjoys the most.

I hold my head up long enough to say, "Let it out, baby, I got you."

"No-o-o-o I'm ready, I'm ready."

That is all I need to hear. Foreplay is over.

Rising up on her, I poke around her pussy with the head of my dick, coaxing it to open. When I feel her body tighten, I keep it right there, gliding it back and forth across her clit. When the sensation is more than she can bear, she spreads her legs, where her oozing cream meets the head of my dick. I don't want to rush it but the blood vessels in my dick have swelled to capacity making me unable to hold back any longer. Her pussy is too warm and too tight. She knows it's coming.

Zinzi holds her breath and I let it all sink in.

Chapter Thirteen

Alpha Male

There were no winners, simply a draw. The infamous Raquel Turner-Cosby has been beaten at a game she created. I've yet to meet or speak with her personally, so far all our negotiations have been handled through our attorneys with Hampton being her new point of contact for The Goodman Firm. Because of that, both Hampton and I are traveling in her private jet on a seven-hour flight to Paris. The purpose, Bilderberg.

Earlier in the week, Tiffany, her children and nanny had flown into Paris under the guise of vacation. On the private plane with them of course was Ms. Turner-Cosby, two of her senior advisors, an assistant and Dante.

Hampton and I arrive at Hôtel Plaza Athénée in the late afternoon. Before checking into my room, I receive a message from Dante to meet Ms. Turner-Cosby at La Terrasse Montaigne, the hotel's sidewalk café.

As the hostess leads me outside to her table, I realize why Avenue Montaigne is the focal point of high fashion and luxury goods. Every imaginable high-end boutique is right in front of me... helpful, I think to myself, as I'd promised to return home with gifts for my mother, Shanté and Zinzi.

It's hard not to miss Ms. Turner-Cosby, who sits wearing a deep blue dress, among the white tablecloths, red chairs and a sea of red geraniums. The only thing that does surprise me is not seeing Dante hovering off in a corner keeping a watchful eye on us... well, actually just me.

When I see her shoulders tighten, I know she feels me coming up behind her.

"Ms. Turner-Cosby," I say, pulling out the chair across from her.

"Don't sit."

Apparently, this meeting will be brief.

I remain standing and her heartless eyes meet mine.

"Mr. Goodman. I've come to realize that whatever is in your best interest, is in *our* best interest."

Finally, she realizes that even though my relationship with these women has enriched my firm, I've never tried to take advantage of her or her daughter; sex with them has been a mere bonus. She's the one who'd showed up threatening blackmail, using me as a gateway to gain access to her daughter, so in that respect she's gotten what she wanted.

"So we're good?"

She nods yes. I walk away.

* * *

Every conference I've ever attended has gift bags loaded with junk that I toss but the swag bag sitting on the desk in my suite is about as high-end as the boutiques across the street.

A black leather brief, embossed with my initials, holds my itinerary for the week, along with a bio on each person I'm scheduled to meet. Next to it sits a large, white Dior shopping bag. Removing the contents, I see that these items have been personally selected for me. On top is a red envelope that holds a $500 gift certificate for the Dior Spa. Under that, is a cedar and leather travel cigar case from Le Lotus and, as if that isn't enough, inside a signature orange Hermès gift box is a grey cashmere and silk scarf. The most surprising gift at the bottom of the bag, under a CD marked Teddy Pendergrass's greatest hits, is a Richard Mille watch.

All of these items have a connection to one person and include a handwritten note.

Bryce,

6:30 am ~ La Cour Jardin.

TJS

Arriving at the courtyard restaurant the next morning, I'm shown to a reserved table under a red umbrella to shade us from the sun. However, this morning the cloudy sky threatens rain. Tiffany enters the garden in a form-fitting, long-sleeve cream dress with a shirred knot on her left hip and another on her right shoulder. She stands statuesque on cognac brown three-inch heels. I know no woman who can look this fine at six-thirty in the morning.

As she approaches the table, I stand up and move to pull out her chair, only to tease myself with the faint scent of her fragrance. When I take my seat, the waiter places a white linen napkin across her lap. She thanks him and I watch her lips that hold only a hint of color and shine.

"Thanks for meeting me so early. It's the only opportunity for privacy," she says, gazing up to the rooms facing the courtyard that are overhung with red geraniums.

"You're the client," I reply, unsure if this meeting will be business or something else.

"I asked you here to...well, I wanted to apologize."

"Not necessary."

As the waiter pours coffee and places a tray of scones between us, I can't help but notice that as much as Tiffany is polished, if I stare at her long enough I'll see the gritty Philly girl who'd been able to take me to the highest peaks of pleasure.

"Dr. Strohmile says my fetish for asphyxiation, combined with the champagne and *other things* had pretty much dehydrated me."

"Other things?"

"Besides the joint..." she smiles, "I added a little something to the bottles of Dom that I thought would enhance the evening."

"I see, and how were you able to keep it quiet?"

"She—" she sips her coffee but her lipstick doesn't leave her lips, "My mother paid them, including the concierge."

"You scared the shit outta me."

"You know she hates you."

"I bet," I respond, wondering if her mother hates me more because I'd chosen her daughter over her that night.

"How are you and your mother?"

"Our relationship is growing. I'm grateful to her, but I won't go public. My parents don't deserve that and neither can my husband's political career afford that attention."

"Have you told them?"

"Yes. After the conference, the Governor and my entire family will be traveling with Raquel and me to our house in Provence. You should come."

"You'd never get to see them."

We both fall silent, her chewing on a scone and me watching her.

"You're dating the woman in my building?"

"Zinzi," I answer, not wanting to reveal any details of the woman I've spent every night with since returning from River Maddox, seduced by her lovemaking and her many delicacies.

"And is it the same with her?" she asks, her eyes searching mine hoping that it isn't.

I choose not to answer because for as much as I enjoy making love with Zinzi, Tiffany's talents are at a level that Zinzi will never achieve. The question is, will it continue to be enough for me.

"Thanks for the gift bag," I say, pushing back my shirt cuff to expose the Richard Mille.

"My appreciation."

"So, what's next for you?"

"I don't know. What would you suggest I do for fun?"

Before I can answer, the waiter interrupts us.

"Pardon me, Mrs. Skinner, your car is waiting."

Just as I'm about to stand up, she says, "Please, stay seated."

Sliding her purse onto her wrist, she comes around to my side of the table, forcing me to look up at her, to smell her, to have my face close to the body that has given me so much pleasure.

Then, in a surprising move she bends over, places her hand against the side of my face and allows her eyes to drift down to my lap. She presses her soft lips against mine and says, "You're a good man, Bryce Goodman. Next time, I'll bring a friend."

Chapter Fourteen

City of Lights

There isn't much downtime during the week, our meetings run from 8 a.m. until 8 p.m. and are interspersed with lunch meetings and receptions, and usually end with a dinner meeting. Ms. Turner-Cosby kept her word, making sure we had the proper introductions with different executives across multiple industries. This trip is giving growth to The Goodman Firm and combined with my personal portfolio, in the next two years, I don't doubt I'll reach my financial goals.

After one especially long day we join Ms. Turner-Cosby, Tiffany and about 50 other people for an eight-course tasting meal at L'Ecrin inside Hotel de Crillon. The incredible cuisine of Chef Christophe Hace has me not only introducing myself to him but also stepping away to share my experience with Zinzi. I'm not surprised that she doesn't answer; the time difference is a killer on our communication. She's incredibly busy with not only the restaurant opening in two days, but also the arrival of her family, who I've put at the Ritz Carlton. I'm pissed that I can't be there for the opening but we both understand the importance of our respective businesses. For that reason we've made a promise to each other that every six months we'll take a long weekend.

When Hampton and I are finally able to slip out of the dinner, I discover that he's reserved us a table at the only Cuban cigar and jazz spot in Paris, Mojito Habana. We spend the next four hours there debriefing about the potential of clients garnered from this trip and of course enjoy the company of Parisian women, who talk to us in French at Hampton's insistence.

At 3:00 a.m. there's a knock on my hotel door. Half-hoping it's Tiffany, I throw the door open. I'm disappointed to find Hampton in a bathrobe holding his iPad.

"What's up? I thought you had company," I say, referring to his earlier statement of not leaving Paris without some French trim.

"Man, this shit made me take a pause," he says. With that, he slides from one screen to the next. I see headlines flash on the screen: On *Philly.com:* "Billionaire First Lady;" *NYT.com* "Daughter of Fortune;" *NYPost.com:* "Love Child Exposed;" *WSJ.com:* "Heir to the Media Throne;" *TMZ.com:* "First Lady Cashes In." There are articles, photos, videos and even memes of Tiffany, her mother, the children; their entire party disembarking from her private jet in Paris.

"How you wanna handle it?"

There's no way I'm getting caught up in this nightmare, as this is one narrative already spinning out of Ms. Turner-Cosby's control. For all I know, she might've leaked it herself.

"Man, I'm getting the fuck outta here. She's got plenty of people to figure this shit out."

"That's it, you good?"

"I'm good."

I jump in the shower, pack my bags and send Ms. Turner-Cosby and Tiffany a joint text.

Me: Might be best if I head back early. Hampton can take things from here.

RTC: Thank you.

There's no response from Tiffany who by now has been joined by the Governor.

By 6:00 a.m. I'm in a Town Car bound for Charles de Gaulle airport. I am hoping to make it home in time for the grand opening of Zinzi's Culinary Institute.

Traveling across the City of Lights, I realize that maybe Zinzi had been right. For the last few months, I'd been spellbound by the raw sexuality of Tiffany and the lure of Ms. Turner-Cosby's billions surely had me captivated. But what Zinzi doesn't realize, is that after tasting her sensual cuisine and virgin body, she's the only one who has me bewitched.

The End

Would you like to know how Bryce became a voyeur? Read *Secret Service*

*   *   *

Note from the author: For those of you who may be reading one of my books for the first time, below I've included an excerpt from my first book and a fan favorite, *Threesome*.

Enjoy!

*   *   *

THREESOME

where seduction, power, and basketball collide

PROLOGUE

May 1998

Sasha

I thought I heard a noise downstairs, but figured it was just my imagination. No need to investigate – it was the same noise I always heard when I was here alone. Always thinking somebody might be sneaking into the house. I didn't have to worry tonight, though, because he was here with me. Maybe not for the whole night, but would be here for a little while. His three, maybe four hours were usually enough to hold me over until the next time. And if someone did enter my home while he was here, then he'd be able to protect me, which is all I really wanted.

But there was the noise again. I lay there hoping it was the house settling, but I knew this old house had long since settled. I turned to look at him; both of us had been unable to say anything since he'd come from inside me. Sometimes it was like that. Our lovemaking was so strong, so intense, that it took our words away, leaving us unable to talk about it until the next day. As I looked at him in amazement I heard the creaking of the stairs. Someone was definitely in the house. Before I knew it, she appeared in my bedroom doorway.

Paulette

I knew they were together tonight. I'd followed him there myself instead of having my cousin do it. I knew the house because I'd slowly driven by it on numerous occasions, once I had all the evidence. Tonight I watched him ring the bell, instead of using his key. The lights were on downstairs, so I could make out through the slightly open blinds her greeting him with a kiss. Then I saw him sit at the kitchen table, and I sat motionless watching her shadow move about fixing his plate.

I'd always known he'd cheated, but I usually reasoned that all men did it, my husband being no exception. I knew he was busy, I mean with two jobs and his various community activities, he was always gone. Things were still the same at home though, the bills were paid and he treated me good, but at times he just seemed happy about something that I wasn't part of.

I mean I had a busy life too. With my job, our son's activities and all the things I was involved in at church, I was often tired and distracted. I knew our marriage wasn't perfect, but it was solid. We had a comfortable home and were part of a decent community. I prayed he would return to church but he continued to profess to being Muslim. I didn't argue because at least he believed in God. My husband was always home for the holidays and each year he would agree to celebrate our wedding anniversary however I chose. But still I noticed.

Then our lovemaking changed. All of a sudden he didn't seem to mind when I didn't want to have sex and often I found myself having to initiate it. And why, I wondered, was he suggesting different things for dinner? Salads, fish, pasta, even dessert when it wasn't a holiday. All the time talking about being healthy, taking vitamins and going to the gym. They were just little signs. Nothing obvious, like staying out all night. I mean once in a while he would come home late, at three or four in the morning, but it wasn't a big deal. What confused me the most was the unobvious. Did he or did he not smell slightly different? It wasn't another woman's perfume, just the faint scent of another woman's aura surrounding him.

Then he upgraded cell phone. I knew he talked to her on the phone at home because his facial expression showed it. I attempted to follow him one day but gave up because I felt stupid and knew that if he noticed me, he would think I was crazy. So eventually I rationalized that I didn't have any real evidence and let it go.

Two years went by and even though his pattern didn't change, I knew he was slipping away. I found myself reading my Bible for answers, yet I would like in lay bed full of anguish, scared to confront him. But I prayed and held fast that the Lord would work it out.

Finally, I needed to be certain. I went to my cousin and explained to him what had been happening. He seemed to know what to do. First he began following Cole, that's when he got her address and a picture. Then he had a friend who worked for Comcast come to our house and put a recording device in the phone. Two months later he came to me with the evidence. It was then that I took the package, went to my mother's house, where I wouldn't be interrupted, and there I listened -- listened to my husband loving another woman.

Cole

After six months with her, I had to ask myself: What the hell was I doing? I knew that I'd gotten in too deep. When I'd met her I thought she might be fun for a little while, like the others had been. Hell, she was single and had her own house on the other side of town. Just what I needed. I'd caught the eyes of a lot of women on the street but something was different about those eyes.

I motioned for her to pull over and she did, but before I could even turn towards her car, she pulled off again. I figured what the hell, jumped into my Suburban and began driving down Broad Street. After only a few blocks I saw her making a U-turn in the gas station, I blew my horn and motioned for her to pull over. This time she parked and I knew the shit was on.

When she stepped out of her car in a brown linen suit, I was impressed with how tall, slender, and brown she was. Not my usual pick of women, who are light-skinned, with long hair and built like shit. No, her hair was natural, full of kinky locs and she had this look of freedom to her. A little makeup maybe but I really couldn't tell 'cause I kept looking at her smile. Once we introduced ourselves I could feel my dick start to get hard. Damn, she was fine.

We found a lot to talk about, except for the fact that I was married. I wasn't about to reveal that, not before I at least had a chance to hit that thing. So we rapped for about an hour, more than I usually did with a strange woman and then she climbed back into her car. As I leaned into the passenger window, she gave me her business card and it was then that I noticed her sliding her long sexy foot out of a brown leather mule. Now, I'd always had a foot fetish; shit, I had over one hundred pairs of shoes and probably even more sneaks. But this foot was beautiful and I was anxious to get those toes in my mouth.

I put her card carefully in my pocket, knowing that Sasha was gonna make my August hotter than my July had ever been.

Sasha

For the first year I didn't even know he was married. A relationship and falling in love were the furthest thing from my mind. I'd just gotten out of a relationship three months before I met him, so all I wanted was someone to take the edge off.

My career was moving on fast-forward as I'd just gone from being secretary to a college dean, to an executive assistant at the high-powered Philadelphia law firm of Mitchell & Ness, whose clients were entertainers and athletes. So I was too busy to realize when he wasn't available. Shit, I couldn't help but be attracted to him. He stood 6'4" tall, with a thick 240 pounds spread evenly over him. But more than that, it was the deep black color of his skin that mesmerized me.

Once I found out Cole was married I was simply too caught up to let him go. I'd tried to end it several times, but each time I was pulled back, with him offering me just enough to keep me right there. I often grew tired of living our relationship inside my house and out of state, when he could get away. I wanted us to be normal and he wanted me to be patient. But nothing could take away those lonely Sunday nights when I'd listen to WDAS FM play ...*Outside Woman, Saving My Love, Agony and Ecstasy, Secret Lover*... all the songs that describe our relationship.

He kept telling me his wife didn't know anything, didn't even suspect. Having been a wife myself, I found that hard to believe, but he insisted. So I figured she was either dumb or didn't care; hell, maybe she had her own thing on the side. Regardless, he was totally unwilling to let me go, yet he was also unwilling to leave his wife. Which I'm not even sure I wanted him to do. I didn't want to see him or his family suffer, so instead I endured the suffering.

Paulette

It would be easy getting into her house. I'd copied her keys from the extra ring he kept on his keychain.

I took the gun off the seat beside me and carefully placed it in my pocketbook. I looked around before I stepped out the car and then glanced up to her window to make sure nobody saw me coming. I didn't care that I'd used my own car, or that I'd parked directly across the street from her house. In the end none of that would matter. The best part was that he had no idea that I knew he was sharing his love with another woman.

As I said a prayer, in an effort to decide if tonight would be my night, the lights went out downstairs, and what appeared to be candlelight began flickering in the bedroom. I hesitated, as the aching in my heart made me want to pound on her door to be let inside. To be let back into the life he'd shut me out of. But no, tonight I would make my move.

I walked past his truck parked in her driveway and onto the porch. Holding the screen door open, I slowly inserted the key; I tried the top lock first but it wasn't locked so I used the doorknob key -- it opened. My hands were shaking and I felt sweat beading up between my breasts -- I was even more determined. I turned the knob and stepped inside.

I was surprised by the house's simplicity. There were dark stained hardwood floors that ran through the downstairs. The living and dining rooms were covered with Oriental rugs that I'm sure were expensive. I could smell her scent of jasmine and spice and unexpectedly I was immediately drawn into Sasha's strange aura, as it had probably drawn in my husband. Yes, I'm sure she had used all these things to lure my husband away. She was no better than Eve, who had tempted Adam.

The house was quiet except for the television, and then I heard it, the sound of my husband snoring. For 14 years I'd listened to that breathing and light choking when he sucked in air too deeply. I started towards the stairs but then changed my mind, no first I wanted to see how she lived. See where he was so comfortable over these last five years that he didn't want to be in our home, except to pass through, as if I were the other woman. Why hadn't he ever told me about her, told me he loved someone else, that he wanted a divorce? No, he just silently kept living two lives. I had to stop myself from thinking too much, so I silently prayed.

Her house, even though simple, was tastefully furnished. I sat down in a chair in the living room, facing a large-screened television, which I'm sure was his favorite spot and I guessed that it was probably here that she sat between his legs. But I couldn't get caught up in that, not right now. There were also plants that filled her home, and fresh flowers that stood on a pedestal. And there were pictures of her grandson.

Then I went into the kitchen. This is where she probably pleased him most. My husband loved to eat and I could tell from the smell that she had been baking. There were dishes on the counter, still covered with food; chicken smothered in gravy, rice, salad, and even a fresh baked apple pie on the counter. I couldn't help but wonder if her food tasted better than mine, so with my fingers I picked a piece of chicken out of the cold gravy and tasted it. Dirty dishes and leftovers, that's how I felt, like a meal he was finished with but couldn't seem to throw away -- well, now he'd have no choice.

I walked back through the dining room, living room, and hesitating at the bottom step, looked up to where all my anguish was coming from. Again, I prayed. As I put my foot on the first step, it squeaked. I held my breath, but realizing it was too late to turn back, I preceded, one step at a time.

I knew her room was in the front of the house. Once I reached the top step, I held onto the banister to brace myself. More family pictures of the two of them -- laughing and happy. Even though my body cringed, I had to admit they even looked in love. But that was my love, my love she'd stolen.

Then I felt it, I felt her sense me, like she knew I'd come. But what she didn't know was what I'd come for. I took the gun from my purse and positioned it firmly in my right hand, removed the safety and placed my finger on the trigger. God will forgive me I told myself.

Initially, I wasn't going to say anything, just do it, but I wanted them to see it happening, and not have a chance to stop me. Approaching the doorway I froze at the sight of the two of them, all cozy and tucked in bed. I wanted to turn away, but no I was doing the right thing. Hadn't I prayed for this night?

What better way for them to pay? They'd hurt me for so long, and Cole actually thought he was getting away with something. Did he really think I didn't know? For once I would no longer be the good girl, it was my turn to be bad.

Cole

Damn, it felt good to be in bed with her. She had no idea how bad I wished I could just up and leave my family. But no matter how much I thought it through, I still came out with the same answer. It was too much work, I had too much to lose. I couldn't walk out on my son, or my wife. Even though our marriage didn't hold any excitement, I still loved Paulette and didn't want to see her hurt. Shit, I even wondered how after all these years she still didn't know. But guess what, I wasn't gonna try to figure it out either. If Paulette could only give me half of what Sasha did, then maybe it would be different at home.

I truly believed Sasha loved me. She knew how to take care her man. Whatever I needed she'd give to me. Backrubs, baths, dinner on the table when I arrived, TV turned to ESPN, slippers by the door, and sex, well I got that any and every way I wanted it. Sometimes it wasn't even the sex, it was just the way she seemed genuinely interested in my life. She believed I could so some of the things I'd lost faith in doing. She was so damn interesting to me; the athletes and celebrities she knew from her job and all that shit she liked; candles, reading, writing and all that back to nature stuff. Sasha wasn't scared of shit. If there was something she wanted to do or try she'd go after it. She had no problem taking risks; hell, I was a risk.

I'd had a lot of women over the years, before and during my marriage but once me and Sasha hooked up I knew she had me because I hadn't fucked with anybody else. Even though I told her I didn't sleep with my wife, I knew she didn't believe me, but what else could I say? But the sex wasn't the same; lovemaking with Paulette was the same as our marriage -- routine. Sasha made me feel like a man. She not only loved me but she loved my body and would examine and make love to every inch of it, even down to my crusty toes. So what was I gonna do --- give it all up?

Having Sasha was better than having a wife. Cause I knew after being with my wife for 14 years that wives didn't give that much. They gave just enough to stay married. That's why I also knew that as much as she wanted me here, if I were to come, to move in, she would change. She'd get comfortable and feel like she didn't have to treat me special anymore. As long as the relationship stayed like this, I could be with her forever and then maybe one day, when my son graduated high school I could make a move. And she knew; she knew I wasn't leaving and didn't often ask except those times when she wanted me so bad she couldn't take it anymore. I knew I was being selfish but the way things were is what worked for me.

Sasha did deserve more --- deserved a man that could be there with her in the morning and be able to count on him coming home every night, someone she could feel like number one with. But what she didn't know is that she was number one with me. I couldn't let her go, I couldn't let her give anybody else what she'd given me. So lying here tonight, after having been drenched in her love, I was in my comfort zone. The way she laid tucked underneath me like a finished puzzle, made me know that she felt the same way.

Sasha

I knew she'd come. No matter how much he denied she had knowledge of us, I knew eventually she would let us know she was no real fool. So here we were, the three of us. Even with the gun in her hand we just stared at each other, knowing it had come to this. I could see through the dimness of the evening light that Paulette was sadly beautiful.

Who would she shoot, Cole or me? Who would she hold to blame, Cole because he was her husband, the one who'd stood before God and made the commitment? Or me because she thought I was some whore breaking up their marriage? I still couldn't move. I called Cole's name, watched his body slowly turn, saw his face look at her, look at me and before I could answer the question in his eyes...

Cole

I know Sasha thought I was sleeping, but her squirming had already woke me, so when she called my name I didn't answer right away. Then I felt Sasha nudge me and I heard my name being called again but this time it was my wife's voice. I turned over to make sure I was hearing right and there she stood. What the fuck was my wife doing in Sasha's bedroom doorway?

As my eyes adjusted to the darkness I could see that not only was my wife there but she was holding my fucking 9-millimeter in her hand. I looked from Sasha to Paulette to ask what the fuck was going on, but before I could say anything, before I could even explain, as if there would be an explanation as to why I was in another woman's bed, the gun went off.

Paulette

Sasha and I never took our eyes off each other while she called his name. When he didn't respond, I called him. He moved, he turned, looked at me, looked at her and before he could ask any questions, I pulled the trigger.

Brenda L. Thomas isn't one to shy away from giving her opinion, after the 2001 release of her bestselling novel *Threesome, where seduction, power and basketball collide*, she subsequently penned *Fourplay, The Velvet Rope* and *Every Woman's Got a Secret*, along with several anthologies.

However, in 2007 Thomas departed from fiction and ventured into the difficult reality of her own past with a deeply moving depiction of her 15 year struggle with domestic violence and drug addiction, releasing her memoir, *Laying Down My Burdens*. As a result of her success, both professional and literary, she appeared on such shows as *CNN*, *ESPN*, Dateline and Entertainment Tonight.

She continues to hone her craft of bestselling author, releasing in 2015 her fifth novel, the African American Literary Award Winner, *Woman on Top*. Then delving into the world of erotica she created a male protagonist, and penned two erotic shorts, *Secret Service* and *Bewitched*.

Currently Thomas is at work on another novel, *Heartless*, set to be released in November 2019. Her favorite past time, besides reading and creating multi-layered characters is spending time with her family and friends, cheering on her hometown Super Bowl Champions, The Philadelphia Eagles.

Contact: www.brendalthomas.com
brendalthomas@comcast.net
215.331.4554

Made in the USA
Monee, IL
18 November 2019